THE LADY IN THE SILVER CLOUD

THE LADY
IN
THE SILVER
CLOUD

A STEWART HOAG MYSTERY

DAVID HANDLER

THE MYSTERIOUS PRESS
NEW YORK

THE LADY IN THE SILVER CLOUD

Mysterious Press
An Imprint of Penzler Publishers
58 Warren Street
New York, N.Y. 10007

Copyright © 2022 by David Handler

First Mysterious Press edition

Interior design by Maria Fernandez

Library of Congress Control Number: 2021921428

ISBN: 978-1-61316-291-0
eBook ISBN: 978-1-61316-276-7

10 9 8 7 6 5 4 3 2 1

Printed in the United States of America
Distributed by W. W. Norton & Company

For Alec Koffman, sole proprietor of the Franklin Typesetting Co. on Franklin Avenue in Hollywood, USA

THE LADY IN THE SILVER CLOUD

CHAPTER ONE

By a simple twist of fate, the single most beautiful automobile in all of New York City was driven by a man who, without doubt, ranked as the honorary captain of the Big Apple's All-Ugly team.

But, please, let me start out by telling you about the car. It was parked at the foot of the awning outside my ex-wife Merilee's luxury prewar apartment house on Central Park West when Lulu and I rode the elevator down to the lobby that day for our regular noon walk in Central Park. This was a regal, gleaming 1955 maroon-and-silver Rolls-Royce Silver Cloud that I'm talking about. Since it was presently 1993 that meant the damned machine was thirty-eight years old, yet it was so spotless it looked as if it had just rolled off the showroom floor. In case you're wondering, 1955 was the very first year that Rolls-Royce decided to phase out the Silver Wraith in favor of the Silver Cloud. Only about 2,200 of them were built, and of those only a fraction were made with left-hand drive for American export. I couldn't imagine that any of them were as gorgeous as this one, which was owned by Muriel Cantrell, an exquisitely delicate, silver-haired lady in her early seventies who happened to be one of Merilee's three sixteenth-floor neighbors.

Muriel had lived there in her jewel box of a one-bedroom apartment since the 1940s. According to Frank the doorman, that made her the building's longest-tenured resident. Muriel was vivacious and extremely set in her ways, Frank had informed me. Mondays she drove to her stylist's salon on West Fifty-Sixth Street to get her hair done. Tuesdays she went shopping either for shoes or for one of the elegant Chanel suits she favored. Wednesdays she took in a Broadway matinee or a movie with her equally classy septuagenarian friend Myrna, who would come into the city for the day from her home in Great Neck, Long Island. Thursdays Muriel visited her lawyer to handle any financial matters that needed attending to. Fridays she drove to Great Neck to play bridge with Myrna and two of Myrna's neighbors.

Mind you, Muriel never drove the Silver Cloud herself. That job belonged to her chauffeur, Bullets Durmond, who was waiting for her on a sofa in his customary black suit, white shirt, and black tie as Lulu and I made our way across the lobby. Paul was his given name, but he was called Bullets by one and all because he'd been shot in the head way back when he was working as a bouncer in Atlantic City—and had a bullet hole in the left side of his forehead and a matching hole on the right side. Same bullet. Somehow, he'd managed to survive aside from a slight stammer, which absolutely no one ever teased him about because even though he was over sixty now, and no doubt slower than he'd once been, Bullets was still six feet four, weighed at least three hundred pounds, and was the owner of the hugest fists I'd ever seen. Also the most battle-scarred face, one that had been on the receiving end of knives, broken bottles, the aforementioned bullet, and enough punches that his nose, which was the approximate size and shape of an Idaho spud, had been squashed so many times that it no longer qualified as a breathing duct. The man was strictly a mouth breather, and so heavy chested and wheezy that I could hear him from twenty feet away. He had cold, heavy-lidded eyes and did not seem to know how to smile. According to Frank, word was that Bullets had been mobbed up for most of his adult life, some of which he'd spent behind bars.

The big man didn't acknowledge my presence as I strolled past him, Lulu ambling along beside me. He never did. As I paused to exchange small talk with Frank at the reception desk, the elevator door opened and dainty little Muriel emerged wearing a pink Chanel suit and clutching a black alligator pocketbook.

"Why, good day, Hoagy," she exclaimed, her big blue eyes gleaming at me. "How are you on this lovely afternoon?"

"Couldn't be better. And you, Muriel?"

"I'm in *the* most wonderful mood," she said, in a voice that had been carefully cultivated to remove whatever trace of working-class accent it once harbored. Lulu let out a low whoop to greet her. Delighted, Muriel bent down and patted her on the head. Her nostrils flared ever so slightly. "I gather you still have her on that same diet." By which she meant 9Lives mackerel for cats and very weird basset hounds.

"I'm afraid so. Just be grateful she doesn't like to sleep on *your* head."

Muriel let out a whimsical tinkle of a laugh. By now Bullets was up on his feet, waiting for her, his tree-trunk arms held out from his sides like a bodybuilder's.

Frank, who wore a formal, six-button, navy-blue doorman's coat and matching trousers, a bellman's cap, and
spotless white gloves, hustled to the front doors and
opened one for her with a tip of his cap, beaming. Frank
O'Brien was in his forties, an apple-cheeked, redheaded
Irish American from Queens who took a ton of satisfaction in being who he was—a third-generation luxury
apartment house doorman and member of the Service
Employees International Union, which was highly prized
for its excellent pay and benefits.

Muriel thanked him as she took her dainty strides
out the door followed by Bullets, who was so wide
that he had to go through the door sideways. Bullets
hustled—or at least tried—to the Silver Cloud's curb-
side back door, opened it for Muriel, and helped her
gently into the charcoal leather back seat. I caught
a glimpse of the burled walnut dashboard as he got
in front and squeezed in behind the wheel. When he
started the engine, it didn't roar. It purred. And off
they drove.

I watched them go as Lulu and I strolled across Central
Park West into the park. Muriel was an intriguing figure
to me. Extremely private, even secretive. Clearly, she had
money, but I had no idea where it came from. All I knew
was that she'd lived by herself on the sixteenth floor since

the 1940s, owned that fabulous Silver Cloud, and had Godzilla for a chauffeur.

I'd asked Frank what her story was. He'd replied, "George, the night doorman, once asked Bullets that very question. Bullets politely asked him to step outside and, after a brief exchange of words, drove his right fist into George's side, fractured three ribs, and bruised his kidney. George was peeing blood for a week. He's never been the same, I swear."

Which I took to mean that George, whose shift ran from 5:00 p.m. to 2:00 a.m., had once been an amiable fellow. He decidedly no longer was. I couldn't get anything more than a sour grunt out of him. I rarely had contact with the building's overnight doorman, Harvey, an old-timer who was nearing retirement. The overnight shift was traditionally the old-timer's shift, since the building's front doors were locked from 2:00 a.m. until 6:00 a.m., which allowed Harvey to doze in peace on a sofa in the lobby unless a late-night reveler came home and tapped on the door to be let in. Harvey didn't really have to be on his feet and alert until 6:00 so as to be of service to early morning joggers, Wall Street titans, and school kids. That was also when a news distributor dropped off stacks of the daily papers, which a high school kid employed by Raoul, the building's super, deposited outside of each and every apartment door by 6:30. Just one of the perks of living in a luxury building. Frank took over at 8:00 a.m. and stayed until George came on duty. On their days off, or if one of them called in sick or went on vacation, the union provided a rotation of backups, usually eager young guys who hadn't yet landed a permanent berth and were anxious to make a good impression.

It was a crisp, cool late October day, one of the best times of year in one of the best cities on earth. The leaves were turning color in the park, about two weeks behind Lyme, Connecticut, where I'd just spent a few days on Merilee's eighteen-acre farm working on my new novel. Or trying to. I ran into a few complications while I was there, including a couple of murders. Maybe you read about it.

Trouble is not my business, yet it always seems to find me.

Which is not exactly what I'd expected ten years back when the *New York Times Book Review* proclaimed me the first major new literary voice of the 1980s in its glowing review of my first novel, *Our Family Enterprise*. I was showered with acclaim and riches. I also met and married Merilee Nash, the gorgeous blonde Oscar and Tony Award–winning actress. We were the city's hottest couple. Lulu even had her own water bowl at Elaine's. But my sunshine days were short-lived. I got writer's block, developed a taste for nose candy, then crashed and burned. When Merilee and I had moved into the luxury building on Central Park West, I'd kept my old, crappy fifth-floor walk-up on West Ninety-Third as an office. It was a good thing I had, because it meant I had somewhere to live when she divorced me. She kept our apartment and the 1958 red Jaguar XK150 that we'd bought. I kept Lulu. At my agent's urging, I'd spent the last decade paying my rent by ghosting celebrity memoirs. I'm not terrible at it. Have three number-one bestsellers to my non-credit. And then last winter—at long last—I got my voice back. Started writing a second novel about *my* New York City, when I was young and wild, the New York City of CBGB, Max's Kansas City, and the Mudd Club. The "FORD TO CITY: DROP DEAD" New York City that teemed with prostitutes, rats, pimps, and gangs. *My Sweet Season of Madness* I was calling it. I'd written the first three chapters over the summer in the guest cottage at Merilee's farm in Lyme, which she'd kindly offered. My agent, the Silver Fox, thought they were not only terrific but had landed me a contract with a hefty advance.

And when Merilee left for Budapest after Labor Day to begin shooting a lavish remake of *The Sun Also Rises* opposite Mr. Mel Gibson, she'd invited me to move back into "our" apartment while she was away. I'd taken her up on it, and for six solid weeks I was up at dawn, head bursting with ideas, fingers tingling to get at my 1958 solid-steel Olympia portable. I'd put on the espresso, crank up the Ramones on vinyl, which was the way it was meant to be played, and get to work in the magnificent office that I'd joyfully discovered Merilee had furnished for me, complete with a signed Gustav Stickley library table, a leather Morris chair for Lulu, and a genuine Hopper oil painting of a craggy Maine landscape for me to stare at when I wasn't gazing out the windows at my panoramic view of Central Park. I was *me* again, right down to my two-day growth of beard, old torn jeans, 1933 Werber flight jacket, and Chippewa boots. I was so into the new book that I did nothing but work. Talked to no one except for Frank and the waiters at Tony's restaurant, my nightly haunt on West Seventy-Ninth Street. After six weeks I'd produced another hundred pages. When I sent them to the Silver Fox, she was even more enthusiastic. "Thrilling" was the word she'd used to describe them.

The autumn air was invigorating as Lulu and I made our way briskly around the rowboat lake. I couldn't remember the last time I'd had such a ton of focused energy. Even Lulu had an extra spring in her step. After nearly an hour, I realized my stomach was growling. I'd forgotten to eat anything that day, which was something

Lulu never did. When I headed back to make myself lunch, I found Frank behind the reception desk talking to Raoul, the building's small, slim, fortyish super, who lived alone in a small ground floor apartment at the rear of the building. Raoul always dressed in a neatly pressed khaki work shirt and trousers. As an added flourish, his name was stitched in red over the left breast pocket.

New York City apartment house superintendents are a special breed. And Raoul, whose family had immigrated to New York from Guatemala when he was a child, was an exemplar of the species, which is to say that he was one slippery little operator. Need a faulty light fixture repaired? Call Raoul. But be sure you've made a healthy advance deposit in the favor bank if you want prompt service, such as a suede jacket, cashmere sweater, bottle of rum, plain old cash . . . Raoul wasn't choosy. He also wasn't above a bit of subtle blackmail. The man *knew* things. Was privy to every naughty secret in the building because he'd personally vouched for and placed practically every cleaning lady, housekeeper, and nanny who worked there, most of them young, undocumented Guatemalan migrants who lived with Raoul's sister in a semidetached house in Astoria. The prettiest of them were expected to provide Raoul with sexual favors. The others kept him supplied him with dirt.

Frank, who was my main source of gossip, had been gleefully sharing with me the latest major dirt about the two other tenants besides Muriel with whom Merilee shared the sixteenth floor. The adjacent park-view apartment belonged to a notoriously ruthless corporate raider out of Harvard Business School named Gary Kates and his rail-thin blonde wife, Olivia Pennington Kates, the celebrated Park Avenue debutante It Girl of the late '70s who now dabbled at fashion design, interior decorating, and her trendy monthly magazine, *Olivia*, which was devoted to the art of how to be as gorgeous and fabulous as its namesake.

Lulu, who has impeccable taste in people, detested Gary and Olivia Pennington Kates. And, yes, it was always Olivia *Pennington* Kates. If Lulu encountered either of them in the elevator, she would growl at them.

Frank had his own reason for detesting Gary, whose most recent corporate raid had bankrupted the venerable national grocery chain that had supplied Frank's unmarried sister with a well-paying union job, complete with health benefits, for the past thirty-two years. As a result, she'd been forced to move in with Frank and his family.

"I'm not the sort who complains about family obligations," Frank had confided in me, "but she's fifty-one, she's lost her health insurance, and now she needs an operation.

Some kind of tumor in her female parts. Guess who has to pay for it. Me. I've got a son who's a freshman at St. John's, a mother-in-law who's in a nursing home in the Bronx. My roof leaks and I can't afford to replace it. I've never had money trouble in my life, but because of that bastard Gary I'm hanging on by my fingernails. How does a guy like that live with himself? Doesn't he realize what he's doing to other peoples' lives?"

"He realizes it. He just doesn't care."

I was telling you about Frank's latest major dirt: The large, airy apartment behind Merilee's, which enjoyed an Upper West Side view all the way to the Hudson River, belonged to Alan Levin, a schlubby little guy with curly salt-and-pepper hair who was a Juilliard-trained pianist and composer. Alan's greatest ambition in life was to be the next Stephen Sondheim, and he'd been composing his debut Broadway musical for so long that I distinctly remember he'd been working on it way back before Merilee kicked me out. But give the guy credit. He was still at it. And he was well connected. His live-in girlfriend, Gretchen, was a production coordinator in the office of her father, one of Broadway's top three producers. Besides, Alan was no slouch. Slouches don't live on Central Park West. He'd made a fortune composing jingles for TV commercials. Chances are that if you'd ever eaten a carton of yogurt, swallowed a bottle of soda pop, flown in an airplane, driven a car, or needed a laxative, one of his catchy jingles had gotten stuck in your head.

According to one of Raoul's sources—Gary and Olivia's housekeeper—Alan's girlfriend, Gretchen Meyer, was about to break up with him and move out because she'd just discovered that Alan had been having sweaty nooners several times a week with Olivia in one of the Kates' guest bedrooms. It wasn't so much that Olivia had an uncontrollable case of the hots for Alan. Harrison Ford he was not. It was more like she was getting even with Gary. The word on the society grapevine was that he was having a steamy affair with the fashion world's hottest nineteen-year-old Brazilian fashion model. They'd met when she appeared on the cover of Olivia's own magazine. Supposedly, Gary had no idea what was going on between Olivia and Alan. *Yet*, I should say. I had zero doubt he would find out soon enough.

"Just the man I wanted to see," I said to Raoul as he stood there at the reception desk with Frank.

"Good day to you, Mr. Hoag," he said in that ingratiating, slightly unctuous way of his. "How may I be of help to you and Miss Nash?"

"The kitchen sink drainpipe has started to drip down into the cupboard below."

"Of course. I'll send for a plumber right away. Anything for Miss Nash. How is she?"

"I spoke to her last night. She said the filming is going great."

"I'm a fan of that Mel Gibson. He's my sort of fellow."

"And what sort of fellow is that, Raoul?"

"If he sees something he wants he takes it—just like that," Raoul said with a snap of his fingers. "I admire such men, don't you?"

It was a rhetorical question, apparently, because he didn't wait for an answer. Just opened the door behind the reception desk and left me alone there with Frank.

Although not for long.

"Oh, hell, *him* again," Frank muttered as someone came in the front door.

I turned to discover that *him* was a pint-sized teen-aged kid, maybe fifteen. I doubt he would have been more than five feet tall if he stood up straight, which he didn't. His shoulders were hunched, his eyes fastened to the floor.

"Who's that?" I asked Frank as the kid crossed the lobby toward us.

"Trevor, the grandson of Muriel's older sister, who passed away. He's a total mooch. Has a major attitude problem, too."

"Need to see my aunt," he mumbled in Frank's direction. His eyes were still on the floor.

"She's not here, son," Frank said politely. "Out shopping."

"Well, then I need for you let me into her place."

"Sorry, I can't do that."

"What does *that* mean?"

"It means no, son."

"Why not?" Maybe fourteen. He was positively whiny.

"Your aunt Muriel has instructed me that I'm no longer to let you in when she's not home," Frank stated firmly.

"Bullshit. You're lying your ass off."

Frank didn't dignify that with a reply. Just stared at him coldly.

I did some staring of my own, because clearly Trevor had more than just an attitude problem. He was deathly pale, with dark circles under his eyes and lesions on his face that he kept picking at in a highly unappealing way. He was also super-hyper and jangly. It all spelled tweaker. He was strung out on crystal meth and desperate to hit up his great-aunt for money. But it sounded as if Muriel was onto him. He must have stolen something of value from her apartment the last time Frank let him in.

"You gonna let me in or not?" he demanded.

15

"Not, as I believe I've made perfectly clear, and if I were you, I'd leave right now before I pick you up by the seat of your pants and throw you out on the sidewalk."

Thwarted, Trevor called Frank a "fucking fuckhead" before he scuttled out, mumbling under his breath.

"Drugs," Frank lamented, shaking his head in his bellman's cap. "They're a terrible thing."

"Tell me something I don't already know."

At Tony's that night, I had pasta with homemade sausages, a side order of spinach sautéed with garlic, and a bottle of Chianti. Lulu opted for her usual calamari. Her mommy's Scorsese movie was playing on the TV over the bar. I parked her on a barstool so she could watch it while I scribbled away in my notepad—the dialogue for one of the scenes I intended to write tomorrow. Scribbled like a madman. I couldn't stop the words from pouring out even if I'd wanted to. And I didn't. After I'd paid the check, we strolled home. I puffed on my nightly Chesterfield that I lit with Grandfather's refurbished Ronson Varaflame lighter.

George, the night doorman, eyed me sourly as we walked in.

"Good evening, George. How are you on this lovely autumn evening?"

"Stuck here in a monkey suit talking to you. How do you think I'm doing?"

"Well, I'm glad to see that you're keeping your spirits up."

He didn't bother to respond. George Strull was a gloomy soul in his fifties with a sallow complexion, vacant eyes, and limp, brown hair that was turning gray. Unlike Frank, who swelled with pride in his uniform, George seemed to shrink inside of his. The jacket hung from his shoulders as if he were still wearing the hanger. His trousers scuffed the ground.

"George is going through a tough time," Frank had told me. "His wife divorced him a few months ago because he's a compulsive gambler. It's like a sickness with him. He keeps betting away his entire paycheck on football, basketball, you name it, and then borrowing money from loan sharks. He also drinks. The two often go together. Or so I'm told. When he refused to get professional help, she gave him his walking papers, kept their nice rent-stabilized two-bedroom apartment up in Inwood, and took up with a new fellow. George is crashing in an illegal basement sublet on West Eighty-Second that Raoul found for him. The same landlord owns four or five brownstones on the block, and Raoul is friends with his super. They scrounged up a bed and a TV for him. That's all he's got. I try to feel sorry for the guy but . . ."

"He's got to take responsibility and get help."

"My feelings exactly, Hoagy."

As Lulu and I waited for the elevator, Gary and Olivia Pennington Kates came breezing in and stood there waiting with us. Gary, who was not lacking in self-esteem, wore a pin-striped suit with suspenders and puffed away on a huge cigar. He didn't bother to acknowledge my presence even though I was living right next door to him. Olivia, who had long, straight blonde hair that she parted down the middle just like Peggy Lipton had in *The Mod Squad*, wore a pair of skin-tight Calvin Klein jeans tucked into snakeskin cowboy boots, a suede shirt, and lots of jangly turquoise bracelets. She did acknowledge my presence. Gave me one of those faint "poor, poor, pitiful you" smiles that were a Gwyneth Paltrow specialty—despite the fact that I was not only the first major new literary voice of the 1980s but was hooked up with a gorgeous movie star who was way more famous than Olivia was. Not to mention the possessor of actual talent.

When the elevator arrived, Gary barged his way in first. Lulu and I stepped aside so that Olivia could precede us.

Neither of them hit the button for the sixteenth floor. That was apparently a job for a lesser sort of person such as, say, me. So I hit sixteen and we rode our way up, Gary continuing to puff on his cigar and fill the car with non-fragrant smoke.

Lulu growled at him.

He frowned at her. "What's your dog's problem?"

"You are."

"I think he means your cigar, Gary," Olivia said.

"No, it cuts a much wider swath than that," I said.

Neither of them responded. Can't imagine why. And they didn't say "goodnight" to me when we parted company at the sixteenth floor. I was so upset I had to make a tear-drenched entry in my diary.

When I unlocked the apartment door and went inside, I found a note on the kitchen table from Raoul informing me that the pipe under the sink had been repaired. I'd have to remember to make a deposit in the favor bank in the morning.

I put down some 9Lives for Lulu in case she got ravenous in the night, then showered and climbed into bed. Lulu sprawled out next to me, somehow managing to take up two-thirds of the king-sized bed. I reached for my notepad and reread the dialogue I'd scribbled at Tony's. Tinkered with it a bit, nodding to myself approvingly. Lay there for a moment listening to the sounds of the city and feeling a tremendous sense of contentment.

For a writer there's no greater feeling in the world than to have something to say again.

I was working my way through a collection of short stories by Wallace Stegner, which is something I do every few years just to remind myself what good writing is. But it wasn't long before my eyelids felt heavy and Lulu was snoring softly next to me. I turned out the light and was soon fast asleep—until, that is, shortly after one o'clock, when Lulu awakened me with a loud whoop, jumped off of the bed, and went skedaddling toward the entry hall, where I swore I could hear keys unlocking the door to the apartment. Now she was whimpering and moaning.

I threw on my silk target-dot dressing gown and staggered my way to the entry hall just in time to discover that Merilee Gilbert Nash, the towering six-feet-tall star of stage and screen, was muscling two large Il Bisonte suitcases and a shoulder bag through the doorway.

I rubbed my eyes. "Am I dreaming?"

CHAPTER TWO

Merilee shut the door behind her and stood there in her long shearling coat, smiling at me wearily. Her waist-length golden hair was gathered up in a bun and tucked in a knit hat. "Do you want me to pinch you?"

"Actually, I had something else in mind."

After I'd helped her off with her coat, I gave her a big hug and a kiss, getting lost in her green eyes.

"Ptui, I should burn these clothes," she complained, by which she meant the charcoal cashmere turtleneck sweater and corduroy slacks she'd been wearing under her coat. "I smell all airplane-y."

"You smell plenty good to me," I said as someone short-legged began howling for attention.

Merilee sat down on the floor so that Lulu could climb all over her, licking her face and making that argle-bargle noise of hers. "Oh, I missed you, too, sweetness," Merilee cooed, hugging and squeezing her. "Not a day went by when I didn't miss your sweet-smelling breath." After she'd made a suitable fuss over Lulu, Merilee raised her eyes to meet mine and said, "I suppose you're wondering what I'm doing home from Budapest. In fact, you even look a teensy bit alarmed."

"Only because I am. I'm terrified that you've been fired for taking your wacky pal Kate Hepburn's advice and telling the director in a loud, clear voice that you're not happy with the rushes you've seen so far, that Lady Brett Ashley doesn't feel *real* to you, and that you intend to *make* her *real*, whether he's on board or not."

Merilee took off her knit hat, tossed it on the floor with her shearling coat, and liberated her shimmering golden hair, shaking it loose and free in a manner that has been known to make male moviegoers gasp audibly. "You'll never guess what just happened."

"This being the movie business, you're right, I won't. Because if I can imagine it happening, if it's reasonable, sane and makes perfect sense, then that's *not* what happened."

"It seems that the suits at Paramount have been watching those rushes for themselves, agree wholeheartedly with me, and . . . cue the drum roll . . . they fired the director."

"No way."

"Yes way. Most decidedly way. Consequently, filming has come to a halt until they can get a new A-list director such as Mike Nichols or Sydney Pollack to take over."

"Is that likely?"

"That would be a no. A-list directors prefer to develop their own projects, not clean up someone else's mess. So I may be home for good. And I'm *starving*. Airplane food is not food."

"No problem. We run a twenty-four-hour kitchen here. While you jump in the shower, I'll fry you up a couple of eggs from the farm, sunny-side up, with buttered toast."

"Bless you, darling," she said, yawning hugely.

I carried her suitcases into the bedroom for her before I turned on the kitchen lights, got out the cast-iron skillet, and dug two eggs and the butter from the refrigerator. While I heated the skillet, I went to work on the loaf of crusty Italian bread that was in the breadbox.

I put the bread in the toaster and flicked it on but waited to put the eggs on until Merilee had returned, all pink and scrubbed, in a cozy cashmere sweatshirt and sweatpants, her wet hair wrapped in a towel.

The eggs made such a mouthwatering sizzle when they hit the hot butter that I cracked two more for myself and stuck another piece of bread in the toaster. Then I set the table and poured us each a glass of milk. Thirty seconds later we were seated at the kitchen table devouring our middle-of-the-night snack. Lulu circled around three times under the table before she curled up on her mommy's feet, grateful to have her home.

"I've been thinking," I said. "If you're back for good then you won't need me to house-sit here anymore. I can pack up and move back to my own place first thing in the morning."

"Are you speaking about that unsightly fifth-floor hovel on West Ninety-Third?" she demanded. "No, sir. I devoted a great deal of time and attention to furnishing that office for you. This is your home. You belong here."

"But I'm laser-focused on my book right now. You may find me to be a bit distant, bordering on grumpy."

"So you'll be distant, bordering on grumpy."

"Plus I'm up at dawn, typing away."

"So I'll be up at dawn, too, getting in my daily jog around the reservoir. I go somewhere almost every morning. I take a dance class, an aerobics class, yoga class . . . And if I do happen to be home, you won't even know I'm here. I'll mute every phone except for the one in the master bedroom. Besides, when I converted that bedroom into an office for you, I purposely chose the one at the end of the hall that's the farthest from the master suite." For some reason the master suite was off the entry hall next to the kitchen. The other bedrooms, four of them in all, had a separate wing off the living room. "*And* I had the carpenter who built your bookcases install a pocket door in the living room that can close off that entire wing. So if you close your office door that'll be *two* doors between us. *Three* if I'm in the master bedroom and close that door as well. Plus I gave you the only bedroom that has its own bath. And if you want a mini fridge or a coffee maker, all you have to do is ask."

"Sounds as if you put a lot of thought into this."

"I most certainly did. I want you back and I won't take no for an answer."

"Merilee, are you sure about this?"

"I've never been more sure of anything in my life—with the possible exception that I was right to turn down the female lead role in *Ishtar.*"

"You won't mind my punk rock?"

"I won't *hear* your punk rock."

"Lulu and I eat dinner every night at Tony's," I warned her. "It's part of my ritual."

She arched an eyebrow at me. "Are you saying that's a deal breaker?"

I considered this for a moment. "I suppose we could, say, try cooking dinner for ourselves a couple of nights a week. Mind you, I may start scribbling notes while we're eating."

"Not a problem. You did that all of last summer when we were having dinner out on the deck at the farm."

"I did?" I tugged at my ear. "That's right, I did."

"Besides, my mind is often elsewhere, too. We've both devoted our lives to navigating our way through imaginary worlds. You create them. I illuminate them. That's one of the things that brought us together and keeps us together. We understand each other. Other people, normal people, don't." Her green eyes sparkled at me. She put her hand over mine and squeezed it. "We're going to make this work, darling. Or die trying."

"Merilee, given my history of dealing with celebrities over these past ten years, I really wish you wouldn't say things like that."

She drank the last of her milk, cleared the table, and got busy on the dishes. "So who's hosting on Sunday?"

"Hosting what?"

"Our floor's Halloween party."

"Oh, that. Haven't the slightest idea."

I should explain that Halloween in a luxury New York City apartment building bears little resemblance to Halloween in the burbs, where costumed kids go marauding from one cul-de-sac to the next, setting off firecrackers, filling mailboxes with shaving cream, pelting passing motorists with eggs, toilet-papering trees . . . Good times. Nothing but good times. Plus there's candy. But in a building such as Merilee's, the poor little rich kids have to go trick-or-treating by elevator. Talk about a drag. To make the occasion a bit less dreary—or more dreary if you happen to be named Stewart Stafford Hoag—one apartment per floor hosts an open house cocktail party from six until eight so that all of the kids can collect their goodies in one place and then be shooed on their way. The host apartment provides cocktails and nibblies. The neighbors bring the candy and are expected to come in costume.

"I'll find out in the morning," Merilee said.

"And what are your more immediate plans?"

"Well, I thought I'd finish these dishes."

"And then what?"

"Apply sixteen different plant-based organic moisturizing emollients, lotions, and oils to my to skin and hair."

"And then what?"

"Brush my teeth."

"And then what?"

"Floss."

"And then what?"

She gave me her up-from-under look, the one that does warm, strange things to the lower half of my body. "Do you have something in mind, handsome?"

"Actually, I have several somethings in mind. I'm an author, you know. Extremely creative."

"I have this vague recollection of hearing something about that. Apparently, your imagination is quite, well, legendary."

"Merilee, there's something I've been meaning to tell you . . ."

"Yes, darling, what is it?"

"Hello."

Her face broke into a smile. "Hello, yourself."

I was up at dawn same as ever, my head bursting with ideas, fingers tingling, raring to hit the typewriter. The only thing out of the ordinary was that I had gotten less than two hours of sleep after Merilee's surprise return in the middle of the night. Not that I'm complaining, mind you. Merilee remained fast asleep on her stomach, a faint Mona Lisa smile on her lips.

And she didn't disrupt my morning routine one bit. I threw on a T-shirt and torn jeans, grabbed my flight jacket and Chippewas and tiptoed out of the bedroom, closing the door softly behind me. Lulu and I went into the kitchen where I put the espresso on and opened a fresh can of 9Lives mackerel. When the espresso was ready, I drank the first cup down practically in one gulp and refilled it. Closed both the living room pocket door and my office door as Lulu followed me in there and climbed into her Morris chair. I stood and sipped my second cup, gazing out the windows at the park. It was a windy, overcast late-October morning and the leaves were completely gone from the trees. Unlike in the country, where autumn lasted for several beautiful, color-drenched weeks, autumn was a two-day nonevent in the city. One day the trees were bursting with leaves. The next day a powerful wind picked up and, shazam, winter had arrived.

I cranked up "Rockaway Beach" good and loud, sat down at my Olympia and was instantly transported back to *my* New York of the '70s and to that brief, precious sliver in time between who I dreamt of being and who I actually became. Back when I was flying high 24/7 and would go anywhere with anyone, day or night. Back when I was utterly fearless and unbound by the slightest moral restraint. We should all have a sweet season of madness when we're young. Now that I'm edging my way into middle age, I can always tell when I meet someone who was too afraid and missed out. They seem joyless and sour now. I feel sorry for them, because that was the greatest time of my life.

Until right now, that is.

I wrote. I was in such a state of ecstatic bliss that the words flew from my fingers. I'd pounded out another twenty pages of first draft by the time Lulu stirred from her morning nap and brought me back to 1993 to inform me that it was time for our noon walk. I lifted the stylus from my vinyl recording of the Velvet Underground and Nico, shut down my stereo system, and we went down the hall to the living room door, sliding it open quietly. There was no sign of Merilee. In fact, the master bedroom door remained closed. She was so jet-lagged she was still asleep.

Out the door we went, my pocket-sized notepad and pen stuffed in the back pocket of my jeans just in case the words decided they wanted to keep on flowing.

Frank beamed at me as we emerged from the elevator in the lobby. "I understand from Harvey that Miss Nash returned in the night."

"That she did. Her movie has been put on hold."

"Well, it's a thrill to have her back."

"It most certainly is. Christmas arrived early this year in Sixteen-B. Just ask Lulu."

Lulu responded with a low whoop, her tail thumping.

There was no sign of Bullets parked hugely on the lobby sofa, wheezing, or of the Silver Cloud parked at the curb, looking fabulous. But I was lucky enough to yet again run into Muriel Cantrell's family burden, Trevor the teenaged meth head, as he came skulking in, sniffling.

"Want to see my aunt," he mumbled at Frank.

"Certainly. I'll see if she's receiving guests," Frank said with great formality. He reached for the house phone on the reception desk and dialed Muriel's apartment. "Afternoon, ma'am. Trevor's here to see you and . . . Uh-huh . . . Right, and what if he . . . ? Okay, I will." He hung up, raised his chin at Trevor, and said, "She doesn't want to see you."

"Bull*shit*."

Frank's pink cheeks got a bit pinker. "Watch your mouth, kid."

"Let me talk to her on the house phone, will ya?" he demanded, his voice cracking. He was even more tweaked and desperate than yesterday. Starting to look like a hollow-eyed zombie.

"She doesn't want to talk to you. She wants nothing more to do with you. So beat it."

"But . . . but . . ." Trevor sputtered helplessly.

"Beat it!" Frank repeated, glaring at him sternly.

Trevor went slinking out in sullen silence.

31

"I hope that's the last we see of that little weasel," Frank said to me.

"It won't be."

"You're right, it won't be. Druggies like him prey on sweet little old ladies like Muriel," he said with a disapproving shake of his head. "Enjoy your walk."

Lulu and I crossed Central Park West, entered the park, and made our way down toward Strawberry Fields and around the rowboat lake. I inhaled the bracing fall air deep into my lungs as we walked. Lulu ambled along next to me, pausing here and there to sniff, snuffle, and snort. My mind was still on what I'd written that morning. Mostly, I was pleased that I'd been able to maintain my focus even though I knew that Merilee was there. Living in the guest cottage on her eighteen-acre farm was one thing. Sharing the same apartment with her was another proposition entirely. But if this morning was any indication, I'd do fine. I wanted to do fine. Wanted it to work out between us this time.

God, did I want it to work out.

When Lulu and I had finished stretching our legs for a good solid hour, we headed back, Lulu speeding up the closer we got to home. She always did that. When we arrived in the apartment Merilee was up and about in an old Yale sweatshirt and jeans, doing domestic things. She'd unpacked her suitcases and stowed them in her closet. Had a load of wash churning away in her fancy red Swedish washing machine in the kitchen. And right now, she was busy putting out a lunch of brie, country pâté, crusty bread, and sliced apples and pears. There was also fresh, hot espresso, which I certainly needed.

But I needed a big, oofy hug even more.

"My goodness," she said breathlessly, her green eyes gleaming at me. "What brought that on?"

"I haven't seen you for hours and hours."

She studied me with great seriousness. "Were you able to get your work done?"

"I was. And Lulu and I got in our daily constitutional in the park."

Her Earness lay there on the kitchen floor, looking rather pooped.

"Me, I just slept and slept," Merilee confessed. "When I finally joined the land of the living, I managed to slip Raoul fifty bucks for getting the pipe under the kitchen sink fixed. He told me that it's Alan Levin who's hosting our Halloween party on Sunday."

I spread some pâté and hot mustard on a hunk of bread and munched on it, sipping my espresso. "Swell."

"Don't sound so excited."

"I hate costume parties."

"Since when? You used to love them."

"I used to love Jerry Lewis and Froot Loops, too."

"I realize you'll need to get up early for work the next morning, so we won't stay long. We just have to be reasonably sociable. Muriel will be in heaven. She loves to listen to Alan play Cole Porter on the piano."

I moved on to an open-faced sandwich of brie and sliced pear. "Will *she* be wearing a costume?"

"I doubt it. Age does have its privileges." Merilee sat down at the table with me, nibbling on a slice of apple. "I also heard *the* most shocking gossip from Raoul. You'll never believe this, but Alan has been—"

"Having a torrid affair with Olivia Pennington Kates. Gretchen has found out about it and is breaking up with him."

"Oh, pooh. You already knew. Who did you . . . ?"

"Frank, who told me Raoul got wind of it from one of his handpicked housekeepers. Apparently, Alan and Olivia have been boinking their brains out in one of Olivia's guest bedrooms for weeks. And Gary doesn't know a thing about it."

Merilee furrowed her brow. "I'm disappointed in Alan, I must confess."

"Why?"

"Because he's got the talent to finish his Broadway musical but he never will if he can be so easily distracted by the dubious pleasures of Olivia, who's nothing but a socialite tramp who'll discard him as soon as she feels like it. Gretchen's a nice girl. She loves him. She believes in him. Plus her father's a major Broadway producer. Now Alan's destroyed all of that. How stupid can a man get?"

"Oh, we're capable of getting plenty stupid."

Lulu stirred, sat in front of the refrigerator, and stared at it, which meant only one thing. I got up and fed her an anchovy, her favorite snack. She prefers them straight out of the fridge because the oil clings better.

"If we *have* to go to Alan's Halloween party," I said, "I suppose I could make a bonus out of it and invite my editor, Norma Fives. She's young, smart, and is desperate to meet you. Plus she can bring her new boyfriend."

"Have you met him?"

"I have."

"Is he nice?"

"Very."

"Is he in publishing, too?"

"Hit rewind. What did I just say?"

"You just said he's . . . Wait, are you telling me you fixed her up with Romaine Very, your homicide detective friend?"

"I'm not sure I'd call him a friend. Strange acquaintance is more like it. And I didn't have to fix them up.

They clicked instantly. Share all of the same neuroses. It's like a match made in heaven. Or somewhere. Anyhow, they've been an inseparable pair of hyperactive brainiacs ever since."

"How sweet. You should definitely invite them." Merilee got up from the table and began clearing our dishes. "Okay, so today's a typical workday for you so far. You've written from dawn until noon in your office. You've taken Lulu for your brisk walk in the park. You've had your lunch. What do you usually do now?"

"I read over my morning's work, hand-edit it, and then retype it."

"Do you usually hand-edit at your desk?"

"No, I usually stretch out on the living room settee."

"You could hand-edit stretched out on the bed just as easily, couldn't you?"

"I suppose. Why are you asking?"

She ran her finger around the edge of my jaw, gazing at me. "Because I was hoping to snuggle with you. I'm starved for affection."

"Well, okay . . . just as long as you understand that this is still the middle of my workday."

"I understand."

"And I really do have to retype those pages before I knock off, understand?"

"Perfectly."

"That means snuggles only. No lingering caresses. No long, slow, wet kisses. No tearing each other's clothes off and having wild-monkey nooner sex. None of that."

She kissed my mouth softly, then not so softly, before she murmured, "Whatever you say, handsome."

CHAPTER THREE

Alan Levin's door was open wide and the man himself was at the keyboard of his grand piano playing Cole Porter's "You're the Top." Muriel Cantrell was seated on a sofa near him, enthralled.

Alan had a big, airy living room with a high ceiling. His décor would have seemed very chic in 1950. In fact, it reminded me of Bette Davis's apartment in the movie *All About Eve*, except that there was no staircase for Alan to descend and proclaim "Fasten your seatbelts, it's going to be a bumpy night."

Which, given what transpired, would have been an entirely appropriate remark.

For one thing, his now ex-girlfriend, Gretchen, a slim, good-looking young woman with shiny black hair who was wearing a loose-fitting cardigan, jeans, and a look of red-faced rage, had purposely chosen the Halloween open house time slot to pack up her possessions and pile them in a small mountain of suitcases and boxes near the front door, pausing periodically to shout "ASSHOLE" at Alan as he sat there tickling the ivories.

Yet Alan was determined to make a festive go of it. For a costume he'd chosen a tuxedo with tails and a top hat, which didn't quite go with his frizzy black hair, goatee, and wire-framed glasses, or the fact that he was no more than five feet seven and decidedly on the chubby side. I couldn't imagine what Olivia Pennington Kates saw in him that had made her want to get naked with him. Maybe she didn't see anything at all. Maybe he was just a handy way of getting even with her husband, Gary, for carrying on with that nineteen-year-old Brazilian supermodel.

Merilee, in salute to her London-based friend Diana Rigg, came to the party decked out in a black leather catsuit and white go-go boots just like Emma Peel used to wear in Diana's 1960s British TV classic *The Avengers*. Sticking with the classic small-screen theme, I came as the ultimate 1950s cool cat Gerald Lloyd "Kookie" Kookson III, the parking lot attendant from *77 Sunset Strip*, which mostly entailed wearing a windbreaker, massaging a half-tube of Brylcreem into my hair, and running a pocket comb through it at regular intervals. That and calling everyone "Daddy-O" or "Doll."

Lulu wore the saucy beret that we'd bought her in Paris, which she reserved only for special occasions.

Since Merilee is extremely fond of kids—which I must confess never ceases to terrify me—she offered to dole out the candy as the building's wealthy young trick-or-treaters emerged from the elevator and found their way to Alan's open door. His was the only one of the four on the sixteenth floor that was open. The sound of his piano helped draw them there, too.

"ASSHOLE!"

For those of you who are curious, a huge purple Barney the Dinosaur costume was very popular that Halloween, as were Batman, Catwoman, Aladdin, and Freddy Krueger. Merilee oohed and aahed and seemed to genuinely enjoy herself with the little monsters.

As added building security, Frank, George, and Harvey Buchalter, the overnight man, were all on duty that evening. Frank manned the lobby, with Bullets seated there on the sofa for company. Harvey ran the elevator so that the kids wouldn't get too rambunctious. George patrolled the hallways to maintain order and pick up the candy wrappers that the spoiled brats discarded on the floor. Raoul kept on eye on the building's service stairs, where the twelve- and thirteen-year-old kids liked to congregate to sneak cigarettes and plot mayhem.

I handed Merilee a glass of champagne as she passed out candy at the door. "Want me to take over, Doll?"

"No need, darling. Why don't you keep Muriel company? She's all by herself."

That was the moment when Gary and Olivia Pennington Kates arrived. Olivia was done up as Glinda, the good witch from *The Wizard of Oz*, who'd been famously played by Billie Burke. Olivia wore a huge pink dress over so many rustling petticoats that she barely fit through the doorway—not to mention wings, a crown, and a pair of mauve-colored kid leather gloves that came up to her elbows.

"Nice costume, Doll," I observed, running my comb through my hair. "But I don't remember Glinda wearing gloves like those." In fact, I didn't remember Glinda wearing gloves at all.

"She didn't," Olivia acknowledged readily. "They're featured in my fall accessories line."

"And you figured this was a perfect opportunity to show them off. Say no more."

Gary was dressed as a pirate, complete with an eye patch and a hook in lieu of his left hand.

"I thought we were supposed to be in costume, Daddy-O," I said to the predatory corporate raider, who wasn't at all amused. In fact, he looked positively furious.

"You'll have to forgive Gary," Olivia said airily, glancing at the mountain of suitcases and boxes behind the door. "As we were strolling over here, I informed him that Gretchen's leaving Alan and filled in the details as to why, up to and including what an attentive, accomplished lover Alan is."

"You shut up!" Gary warned her angrily.

But Gretchen was not to be outdone. "SLUT!" she snarled at Olivia as she deposited another suitcase by the door. "I can't believe you had the nerve to show up here!"

Olivia stuck her pert little debutante nose in the air and remained silent. She wouldn't dignify such a remark with a response, especially when it came from a lesser being.

"And *I* can't believe I let you drag me here," Gary said between gritted teeth.

"So why don't you leave?" Olivia said with a wave of one of her mauve-colored kid leather gloves.

His eye—the one that wasn't covered by the eye patch—narrowed to an angry slit. "You'd like that, wouldn't you?"

"Frankly, yes."

"You've actually been shtupping that fat little putz?" he demanded as if Merilee, Gretchen, and I weren't standing right there in the doorway hearing every word he was saying, along with assorted Barneys, Catwomen, and Freddy Kruegers.

"He's sensitive, gifted, gentle, and he adores me," Olivia responded defiantly. "That makes four things right off that you aren't. Or don't."

"Cool it, kids," I said to them. "You're puttin' a foggin' in my noggin."

"Oh, go to hell, Hoag," Gary blustered at me.

Lulu immediately let out a growl, baring her teeth at him.

"What's *her* problem?" he demanded.

"She doesn't like it when pirates say nasty things to me."

"Well, that's just too fucking bad."

"I've enjoyed this little chat," I said to him pleasantly. "You and your lovely wife are a slice of heaven. And there's truly nothing like a Halloween open house to lift one's spirits, is there?"

I decided to pour myself a Glenmorangie single malt Scotch from Alan's butler's tray, join Muriel on the sofa, and savor Alan's mastery of Cole Porter. Muriel had to be the most delicately exquisite woman over the age of seventy I'd ever met. Her eyes were a twinkly China blue, her complexion smooth and creamy. Her silver hair, cropped becomingly at her chin, positively gleamed. She was decked out in a handsome black Chanel suit and a string of pearls and was clutching a small alligator pocketbook. She smelled faintly of lilac bath soap, not perfume, which was just as well. Lulu is allergic to most perfumes. Sneezes her head off.

"My, aren't you the young hooligan, Mr. Hoag," she said brightly.

"Make it Hoagy, Doll," I said, reaching for my pocket comb.

She let out a delighted cascade of laughter. "I'm trying to remember the last time anyone called me 'Doll.'"

"And . . . ?" I asked her.

"I'm afraid I can't," she lamented. Muriel was very practiced at the art of being charming without ever revealing a thing about herself. All of which made me even more curious about her past life. "This is a very exciting evening for me," she said. "My dear friend Myrna and I are going to take in Bobby Short's ten forty-five show at the Café Carlyle."

"You are in for a real treat indeed."

"I can't wait. Myrna hates Halloween parties, so she's currently at the Loews multiplex on Broadway and West Eighty-Fourth watching *Sleepless in Seattle* for the fifth time. She loves that movie. Sobs every time. Bullets drove out to Great Neck to fetch her and drop her off there. He's waiting for me downstairs now. We'll pick Myrna up at eight thirty and he'll take us to our favorite Chinese restaurant, Szechuan Gardens, on Broadway up near One Hundredth Street. Myrna swears you can't get decent Chinese food in Great Neck. Then it's on to the Carlyle to see Bobby." She trailed off as Alan segued into "Begin the Beguine." "I can imagine Alan playing at the Carlyle himself someday, can't you?"

"He has the talent," I acknowledged. "But you need more than talent to become as accomplished an entertainer as Bobby Short. You need drive and determination. Also someone who believes in you."

Muriel raised one eyebrow ever so slightly. "Such as Gretchen, you mean. And he's driven her away. I don't blame him. A chubby little fellow like Alan can't help himself when the likes of an Olivia Pennington Kates throws herself at him. It's Olivia whom I blame. She's bad to the bone, that one." Muriel glanced over my shoulder at Olivia, who was still near the doorway chatting with Merilee. "Ironic, isn't it, that she came as Glinda the Good Witch? She's so much better suited to being the Wicked Witch of the West."

"Possibly the green makeup clashed with her mauve-colored gloves. They're featured in her fall accessories line, you know."

She let out another cascade of laughter. "You're a terribly naughty boy, Hoagy."

My young editor, Norma Fives, and Detective Lieutenant Romaine Very appeared in the doorway now with the latest batch of trick-or-treaters.

I asked Muriel to please excuse me and went over to greet them. They were not, strictly speaking, wearing costumes, but their normal, everyday outfits more than sufficed. Norma was a scrawny, hawk-nosed little woman with thick horn-rimmed glasses and a blunt hairdo that looked as if she'd cut it herself in the bathroom mirror with a pair of poultry shears. Toss in the boxy, short-sleeved knit dress she had on and Norma bore an eerie resemblance to one of those nutso, skinny-armed little girls in Roz Chast's brilliant *New Yorker* cartoons. She seemed more than a bit overwhelmed as she gazed up, up, up at the great Merilee Nash in her Mrs. Peel catsuit and go-go boots.

As for Detective Lieutenant Very, who, like Norma, was in his late twenties, he looked like a skater punk in tight jeans, a tight black T-shirt, and black leather jacket. Very had a lot of thick black hair, three or four days of stubble, an earring, and those soft, soulful brown eyes that women get woozy over. Olivia certainly did. She hadn't taken her eyes off him from the second he walked through the door. I doubt that Very stood more than five feet six, but his biceps and pecs rippled and his thigh muscles bulged. He had such an air of hyperintensity that he often nodded his head rhythmically as if he heard his own speed-metal rock 'n' roll beat. He chewed bubble gum at high speed, too. Glancing at him, it was hard to believe that he had a degree in astrophysics from Columbia and was a cop. Unless, that is, you caught sight of the SIG Sauer P226 semiautomatic that was tucked in the shoulder holster under his snug-fitting leather jacket.

Lulu, who loved him, let out a low whoop and rolled over on her back, her tail thumping. He knelt and made a fuss over her before he stood back up and shook my hand. "Good to see you, dude."

"Right back at you, Lieutenant."

Very worked homicides out of the Twenty-Fourth Precinct on the Upper West Side. Officially, that is. Unofficially, he was the top homicide cop in the entire city, especially when there were famous people involved. Because of my non-chosen career as a celebrity ghostwriter, our paths had crossed several times—most recently because of a manuscript by the incredibly popular novelist Addison James that went missing and the murders that had occurred in its wake. Very possessed a rare combination of brains, instincts, and guts. It also didn't hurt that his rabbi was none other than Inspector Dante Feldman, the man who'd caught Son of Sam and was now the commanding officer of all of Manhatttan's homicide detectives.

There was a bucket filled with bottles of Molson ale on ice on the dining table. Very opened one, took a sip, and said, "I'm thinking this could be the first time I've ever run into you when we weren't standing over a dead body together."

"You may be right about that. Makes for a nice change of pace."

"I could get used to it."

Norma joined us and gave me an awkward, elbowy hug. "She's just like a regular person. You'd never know that she's *the* Merilee Nash!"

"Thanks for coming. I wasn't sure I could drag you out of your office," I said, since Norma was a world-class workaholic.

"Are you kidding me? You think I'd miss a chance to see you in the flesh? You told me you'd be low maintenance. You didn't tell me you'd disappear off the face of the earth. I have authors who call me practically every day. One of them calls me in the middle of the night, sobbing. You haven't called me *once*. You haven't shown me pages. All I know about your book is what I hear from Alberta, who told me the latest hundred pages are thrilling. How come you've let *her* see pages and not me?"

"Because I've known her forever and she's always been my first reader. When I show it to you, I don't want it to be a work in progress. I want it to be the best that it can be without the help of a gifted editor."

"But I feel as if I'm not contributing."

"You'll contribute big-time when I'm ready for you, trust me. Would it make you feel any better to get a look at where I work?"

Norma let out a gasp. "Are you kidding me?"

I led them toward the door, where Merilee was handing out candy to a runt-sized New York Rangers goalie. "We'll be right back. I want to show Norma my office."

"By all means, darling. And, listen, this will only last until eight. Why don't you folks stay and have a light supper with us? I'll throw something together."

"That would be awesome, Miss Nash," Norma responded excitedly.

"Norma, if you don't start calling me Merilee I'll have to slug you."

"And she has a wicked right hand," I said. "So watch yourself."

Lulu escorted us home. I unlocked the apartment door and showed them in, flicking on a few lights.

Norma froze in the marble-floored entry hall, gazing first at the signed Stickley tall clock and umbrella stand, then at the dining room with its hexagonal dining table with six matching V-backed chairs. And, lastly, at the living room with its floor-to-ceiling windows overlooking Central Park and its settee of oak and leather and two Morris armchairs.

"I-I can't believe how beautiful this is . . ." she gasped.

"Pretty amazing, isn't it? I really missed it when she gave me the boot. For the past ten years Lulu and I have been banished to a fifth-floor walkup on West Ninety-Third that's a total—"

"Shithole, I know. Romeo told me all about it."

"Well, he would know. He's been there quite a few . . ." I glanced over at him, frowning. "Sorry, what did she just . . . ?"

Very reddened. "She calls me Romeo."

"And he calls me Baby Girl," Norma said, linking her arm in his.

"I'm incredibly happy that the two of you found each other, and you're safe with me, but I wouldn't use your pet names around other people. They might fwow up."

Norma looked at me curiously. "Don't you and Merilee have pet names for each other?"

"No. Well, yes, she calls me Fabio—but never outside of the bedroom."

"I want to see your office now," she said firmly.

"Sure thing, boss."

Very, who was no stranger to Merilee's apartment, remained behind to take in the view from the living room.

"He sure admires you," Norma said as Lulu and I led her down the hallway. "He said you have the keenest detecting mind he's ever come across."

"Very said that?"

"Except he's still not sure how much is you and how much is actually Lulu."

"Oh, that. Yeah, we're a team, like Moose and Squirrel." On her blank look I said, "Not a big *Rocky and Bullwinkle* fan, I take it."

She stopped cold in the office doorway, awestruck by my view of the park outside of the windows. And by my built-in floor-to-ceiling bookcases filled with not only books but my stereo and extensive collection of '70s vinyl. And by the Stickley library table that served as my desk. "I can't *believe* this is where you work." She ran a finger over my Olympia, which was parked facing the windows. "Gawd, this is like my fantasy office."

"Trust me, it's mine, too."

Norma gazed longingly at the stack of manuscript pages that were heaped on the table.

"No peeking," I said to her.

"You're a meanie."

"That's me, all right."

She pulled her eyes away, peering at the Hopper that was hanging over Lulu's chair. "Is that . . . I mean, *real*? As in not a print?"

"Take a wild guess."

"Gawd."

We started back toward Very in the living room. Lulu, who was just getting settled in her chair to take a nap, grumbled but followed us.

As it happened, it was fortuitous that Romaine Very was on hand for Alan's Halloween party, because we returned to find Alan and Gary Kates rolling around on the floor throwing punches at each other. Pudgy little Alan's left eye was swollen shut, and he had a bloody fingernail nail gouge over his right eyebrow but was giving as good as he got. Gary had a bloody nose and was bleeding from the mouth.

Gretchen was weeping. Olivia was watching with savage glee. Merilee was just standing there shaking her head in disbelief.

"Okay, cool it, tough guys!" ordered Very, who stepped in, picked up Gary by the shoulder of his pirate costume, and tossed him aside like a rag doll. Those muscles of his were not just for show. "What's this all about?" he demanded as the two combatants lay there, gasping and bleeding.

"It's a personal matter." Gary wiped his bloodied mouth with a handkerchief. "And none of your damned business."

Muriel fetched Alan a dishtowel from the kitchen for his bleeding forehead. "Here, dear. You don't want to ruin that lovely white shirt."

"I want you two chowderheads to shake hands," Very said. "Right goddamned now."

"No way," Alan said fiercely. "Not going to happen."

"If you don't then I'm running you both up to the Twenty-Fourth Precinct house for disturbing the peace."

"What, you're a cop?" Gary demanded.

"That's the general idea." He flashed his shield. "Detective Lieutenant Romaine Very."

"You're an actual detective?" Olivia's eyes widened with wanton interest. "How much of a turn-on is that?"

Which prompted Norma to say, "Back off, Blondie. He's *mine*." Norma was scrawny, but fierce. She'd once hurled a Stanley Bostitch stapler across a conference table at her boss and nearly blinded her.

"I'm still waiting for that handshake," Very said, his jaw muscles working on a fresh piece of bubble gum.

The two of them shook hands grudgingly.

"That's more like it."

Raoul appeared in the doorway and announced, "It's eight o'clock, folks. We're putting a lid on the trick or treating. Thanks for . . ." He broke off, glancing from one rich, bloodied resident to the other. "Hey, is everything okay in here?"

"Everything's under control," Very assured him.

Gretchen said, "Raoul, I'm going to need someone to help me lug my things down to the lobby."

"Certainly, Miss Meyer. I'll see that it's taken care of as soon as I stop in at the other floors."

And on that cheery note the residents of the sixteenth floor returned home to their respective apartments. Muriel thanked Alan profusely for hosting the open house before she started down the hall, clutching her pocketbook. Gary and Olivia didn't bother to thank Alan. Merely left, glaring at each other.

After Merilee had thanked Alan, she gave Gretchen a sympathetic hug and said, "Call me if you want to talk."

Gretchen ducked her head, nodding.

Lulu and I started back to the apartment with Norma and Very.

Merilee caught up with us. "Now, remember, I can't promise you anything fancy. Just a frittata and a salad."

"What's a frittata?" Norma asked Merilee as I unlocked the door and we went inside.

"It's like a giant omelet with potatoes and onions and whatever else you can find in the refrigerator. I think I saw some roasted peppers in there. Would you like to help me make it?"

"I have zero idea how to cook," Norma stated flatly.

"Then tonight you shall start learning." To me she said, "Would you like to fetch our guests some drinks? I need to get out of this costume so that I can actually breathe." She paused to help Lulu off with her beret, which had its own peg in the hall closet, then off she went to change clothes.

Very wanted a Bass ale, as did I. Norma asked for a glass of Chianti. I knew that Merilee would want a glass of Chianti, too, just as I knew that Lulu would want an anchovy as soon as I opened the refrigerator door.

By the time I returned to the living room with the drinks on a tray, Lulu had joined Very and Norma on the settee, where our young guests sat gazing out at the view, transfixed. Merilee soon came in and curled up in an armchair wearing jeans and a soft, old olive-green moleskin shirt that had been mine until about two minutes ago. Merilee loved to steal my cozy old shirts. I didn't mind. It made her happy. Besides, they looked ten times better on her than they did on me. After I'd distributed the drinks, I sat in the other armchair and took a gulp of my Bass.

"So what was that fight all about?" Very asked me.

"It seems that Olivia Pennington Kates, the skinny blonde, has been having a fling with Alan, the pudgy pianist, to get back at her husband, Gary, for having a fling with a supermodel."

"Gary Kates . . ." Very thumbed his stubbly chin. "Isn't he that corporate raider?"

"One and the same."

"Dude's human scum. Cost my uncle his pension."

I nodded. "One of the doormen, Frank, was telling me that Gary cost his sister her job. A single woman who'd been working for the same grocery store chain for thirty-two years. Now she's had to move in with Frank and his wife, needs an operation, and has no health insurance."

Norma sipped her wine. "How do people like that live with themselves?"

"I often wonder about that myself," I said.

Merilee gazed at me with her shiny green eyes. "And where has your wondering taken you?"

"I think they truly, deeply believe that everyone else in the world is as venal as they are. That what they do is normal, everyday business and they're simply better at it than other people are."

Merilee nodded. "I also think they don't give a damn about those other people."

"Well, there's that, too."

"She looked familiar," Very said. "The skinny blonde."

"Olivia was an It Girl," Merilee said to him. "A famous Park Avenue debutante. Now she's a socialite fashion designer and publishes her own magazine."

"I hate her sort," Norma fumed. "When I was in high school, they used to make fun of my body in gym class. They were incredibly mean. One of them even put a live mouse in my locker. But I got back at her."

"How?" I asked with keen interest.

"I corralled the mouse and stuffed it in her book bag. When she got home from school, it jumped out and started running around on her bed. She went into such hysterics that her mom had to rush her to the hospital to be sedated." Norma smiled contentedly at the memory. "It was way cool."

"You truly *were* born for a career in publishing, weren't you?" I said admiringly.

She turned to Merilee and said, "I *love* your apartment."

Merilee smiled. "It's homey, especially now that I'm not living here all alone anymore." Lulu's tail thumped. Mine would have thumped, too, if I had one. "Are you ready to learn how to make that frittata?"

Norma followed her shyly into the kitchen, still awestruck that they were going to hang out and cook together.

"So how goes it with you crazy kids?" I asked Very.

"I'm nuts about her," he confessed. "She's wicked smart. She's funny. We talk for hours and hours about everything and nothing. It's also the best sex I've ever had, I swear."

"I want it noted that I didn't bring that up, as it were."

"Duly noted. I just can't figure it out, dude. I mean, Uma Thurman she's not. But none of that matters. When we're between the sheets it's like we've got this incredible chemistry."

"That's a rare thing. I'm really happy for you."

Someone knocked on the door. It was a frantic knock. Lulu let out a bark. She has a mighty big bark for someone with no legs. Jumped down from the settee and went scampering to the door. When I joined her there and opened it, I discovered it was Raoul.

The building's super was so upset he was shaking. "I'm so terribly sorry to bother you, Mr. Hoag," he blurted out. "But I was told by Mr. Levin that a police detective and his lady friend joined you and Miss Nash after his party broke up. Is he still here, by any chance?"

"Yes, he is. Why?"

Very, who'd heard every word Raoul had said, joined us in the doorway. "What can I do for you?"

Raoul gulped. "I helped Miss Meyer load her possessions into a taxicab and sent her on her way. The poor woman was crying," he said, his words tumbling out nervously. "After that I began tidying the service stairs. Bagging up the candy wrappers and cigarette butts that the kids left behind. I started at the first floor and worked my way up. When I reached the fifteenth-floor landing, I . . ." He broke off, fighting to hold on to his composure. "I found Muriel Cantrell lying on her stomach there on the cement floor in her lovely black Chanel suit with her head twisted at a strange angle. Her face, it's . . . it's like her cheekbone has collapsed. Her eyes are wide open. She's *dead*."

"Let's go have a look," Very said, patting him gently on the back. "Which apartment was hers?"

"Sixteen-D. It's toward the rear, not far from the stairs."

He led us to the door to the service stairs, which doubled as the emergency fire stairs. They were tucked toward the rear of the floor behind the elevator shaft. Muriel's apartment door, which was closed, was less than ten feet away. I handed Very a handkerchief, which he used to open the door to the stairs, leaving it propped open with the kick-down doorstop. We stood there at the top of the stairs and looked down. Muriel was as Raoul had described her—lying facedown on the fifteenth-floor landing with her neck craned at an exceedingly unnatural angle. Her nose had bled a little. Not much. One shoe was still on, the other half off. They were low heels. Not the teetery sort.

"The poor, dear lady," Raoul said quietly. "Such a nice person. So generous, too. Gave me a thousand dollars in cash every Christmas. Gave the doormen very nice cash bonuses, too. She always paid everyone in cash. Her housekeeper, anyone who did work for her. Never wrote a check. Just like in my old country. I can't stop talking, I'm sorry. I get this way when I'm upset. What do think you happened, may I ask?"

"Broke her neck," Very said. "Probably the C1, 2, and 3 vertebrae. It's an instant death. The respiratory nerves are severed and you stop breathing. She hit with great velocity, which would account for the way her face looks. The medical examiner will have to determine if there are any leg or hip bruises, but, offhand, I'd say one of two things happened. Either she was taking the stairs down to another floor and tripped and fell, or . . . "

"Or . . . ?" I asked.

"Or someone grabbed her in the hall when she was heading back to her place from the party, yanked her into the stairwell, and shoved her down the stairs."

Lulu was sniffing her way carefully around the carpeted hallway outside the doorway, snuffling and snorting. I don't just keep her around for her looks. Bassets are keen scent hounds. Second only to bloodhounds in the canine universe. But she had nothing to offer so far.

60

"Muriel was carrying a small alligator pocketbook," I said. "I don't see it. Did you come across it, Raoul?"

Raoul shook his head. "No, sir."

"How about the keys to her apartment?"

Again Raoul shook his head. "No, sir."

Very gazed at me. "You thinking it was a robbery?"

"If she always paid cash for everything, that means she always carried cash. The keys to her apartment would have been in her pocketbook, unless she'd already taken them out."

"Do you have a spare set of her keys?" Very asked Raoul.

"I do."

"We'll have to access the apartment to determine if she was robbed."

"Absolutely."

"You said she had a housekeeper?"

Raoul nodded. "Rosalita. She comes twice a week to vacuum and clean. Also to do her laundry and ironing. She lives with my sister in Astoria."

"Get Rosalita over here right away. She might be able to tell us if something's missing."

"Of course. Whatever you say, Lieutenant. She's a nice girl. Good girl."

Me, I wondered if she was also one of the ripe young fruits on Raoul's little yum-yum tree. I also wondered if he'd found the pocketbook when he found Muriel and stashed it in his apartment before he came knock, knock, knocking on Merilee's door. Totally on the straight and narrow Raoul was not. "Is Muriel's chauffeur still here?"

"Bullets? Yes, sir. He's been waiting for her down in the lobby."

"Any idea why?" Very asked.

"Muriel told me why at the party," I responded. "She said that her friend Myrna hates Halloween parties, so Bullets drove her over to the Loews on Broadway and West Eighty-Fourth to see *Sleepless in Seattle* while we were yukking it up at Alan's. She and Myrna had planned to go out to dinner afterward and then catch Bobby Short at the Café Carlyle. Raoul, does Bullets know about this yet?"

Raoul's eyes widened with fright. "Good God, no. I didn't dare tell him. I came to look for the lieutenant first thing."

"You did good," Very said. "I'll be the one to tell him. But first I have to phone it in."

"And I'll call my sister and tell her to put Rosalita in a cab," Raoul said. Should I do anything else?"

"Just make sure no one uses these stairs. Have one of the doormen stand guard until I can get a patrolman here."

"Of course, Lieutenant."

We started back to the apartment so that Very could phone it in and we could tell Merilee and Norma that they'd have to enjoy their frittata without us.

"Turns out I spoke too soon, dude," he said to me in a grim voice.

"How so?"

"We did end up standing over a dead body together."

CHAPTER FOUR

Bullets didn't exactly take the news of Muriel's death well.

The big man erupted with an animal roar when Very told him, struggled to his feet, and drove one of his giant fists through the lobby wall, which I imagined would make for a very expensive repair job to the wall. Didn't seem to do any damage to his hand. It took the combined strength of Frank, George, Very, and the first major new literary voice of the 1980s to settle him back down on the sofa, his chest heaving as two blue-and-whites pulled up out front, their tires screeching.

When Very had phoned it in from Merilee's apartment, she and Norma were in the kitchen, frying onions and chatting away.

Merilee was so heartbroken over the news that her green eyes pooled with tears right away. "That poor dear. She was such a sweetie."

I put my arms around her. "I know."

"This is just awful."

"I know."

Very said that he was sorry he wouldn't be able to stay for dinner. That went double for me. Merilee insisted that Norma stay and eat with her.

"Are you sure I won't be a bother?"

"Absolutely not. You're Hoagy's editor. I want to get to know you better."

"Well, okay. I mean, I would love that."

Very gave Norma a kiss on the forehead. "Gotta jet. It's going to be a long night. I may not make it home before dawn. In fact, I may not make it home at all."

She hugged him tightly. "Be careful."

And now we were down in the lobby trying to grapple with a freaked-out sixty-something giant. Two of the patrolmen helped out. Very ordered the other two to cordon off the stairwell doors on the fifteenth and sixteenth floor and to stay put there. Harvey, who'd been standing guard until they arrived, was now relieved of duty.

"I g-gotta make a phone call!" Bullets roared at Very. "Phone call!"

Frank gestured to the phone on the reception desk, "There's one right here."

"Not here! In p-private!"

Frank looked inquiringly at Very, who gave him a brief nod. "We have a break room through that door behind the desk. You can use the phone in there."

Bullets lumbered through the door behind the desk, slamming the break room door shut behind him. A moment later I heard his raised voice on the phone. The only words I could make out were "I d-don't fucking know n-nothing!"

While he was making his call, I stood there at the reception desk with Frank, George, and Harvey. Lulu seemed particularly interested in the cuffs of George's navy-blue doorman's trousers, sniffling and snuffling at them.

"Tell her to cut that out," George grumbled at me.

"I never tell her what to do. She's a free agent."

"Okay, have it your way." He kicked her—hard enough that she let out a yelp of pain.

"Whoa, butthead!" I grabbed George roughly by his jacket lapels as Lulu cowered behind me, whimpering.

"You ever do anything like that again and I'll rearrange your face so that no one will be able to tell you and Bullets apart."

"You and who else?"

"I won't need any help. Shall we step outside right now?"

"I've never liked you, Hoag," he said bitterly.

"I know, and it's always been a great source of hurt. Your respect would mean so much to me. So are we stepping outside or do you only go after smaller animals?"

George glanced over at Frank, who was glaring at him. So was Very. The two cops in uniform, both young, were glaring at him, too. "Okay, here's the deal," he confessed. "I was bit in the ankle by a stray dog in the street when I was a kid. No tags or nothing. So I had to go for rabies shots—in the stomach."

"That must have been traumatic."

"It was." He studied the floor, unable to look me in the eye. "And I, uh, apologize."

"Apology accepted," I said, releasing my hold on his jacket.

Bullets finished his phone call and barged his way back through the doorway. "Gotta go p-pick up Myrna," he blustered. "She'll be waiting outside the m-movie theater for me. Gotta go!"

"You're not going anywhere, big fella," Very said to him calmly. "I'll send these patrolmen to pick her up and take her home."

"But she lives in a c-castle way out in Great Neck."

"So they'll take her to her castle way out in Great Neck. What's Myrna's last name?"

"Waldman."

"And what does she look like?"

"She's in her in m-mid-seventies but you'd never know it. Tall, slim, black hair. Real well p-put together. C-Classy, know what I mean?"

"Go pick her up," he said to the young patrolmen. "Be respectful and courteous. You're about to break it to her that her best friend just fell down a flight of stairs and died. If she asks, tell her that Bullets was asked to remain at the scene as a witness. Myrna is elderly. Make sure she's seated when you give her the news. Got a first aid kit in your cruiser?"

"Sure thing, Loo," one of them said.

"Good. No jibber-jabber from the front seat on the way out to Great Neck. Nothing but respectful silence, understand? Now get going." Out the door they went. Then Very turned to Bullets, his jaw muscles working on a fresh piece of bubble gum. "Have a seat."

"What f-for?"

"Because I told you to."

"Want to see your shield."

"No prob." Very dug it out of the pocket of his leather jacket and showed it to him.

"Think m-maybe I heard of you," he said grudgingly as he lowered his bulk back down onto the sofa. "You're a homicide guy. Get your name in the p-papers a lot. Why are *you* here?" He began mouth-breathing more heavily, his huge chest rising and falling. "You telling me Muriel d-didn't trip and fall on those stairs?"

"That'll be up to the medical examiner to determine, but it looks to me as if somebody shoved her down the stairs. Plus her pocketbook's missing."

Bullets's eyes blazed at him. "You k-kidding me?" he demanded.

"I wouldn't kid you. There's nothing funny about murder." Very pulled a small notepad and pen from his jacket pocket. "What's your full name, Bullets?"

"Durmond. Paul Michael Durmond."

"Where do you live?"

"In Rego Park with m-my sister, Rose. The house we g-grew up in. We inherited it when the folks died. She's single same as me. We share it."

Very handed him the notepad and pen. "Address and phone number."

He took the pad and pen, slowly scrawling down the information with his huge hand before he passed it back to him.

"Have any priors, Bullets?"

"I got nothing t-to say about that," he answered gruffly.

Very let out an exasperated sigh. "We can do this one of two ways. You can answer my questions here and now so you can go right home to Rego Park, or I can transport you to the two-four and put you in a holding cell overnight while we run a criminal background check on you and then question you in the morning. So let's try a do-over. Have any priors, Bullets?"

"Do I n-need a lawyer?"

"That's not for me to say. It's just an inquiry at this point. Mind you, if you're the one who pushed Muriel down the stairs and stole her pocketbook . . . "

"I'm n-not, I swear! Sat right here all evening and never budged. I just d-don't like to talk about the old days, that's all." He ran a giant hand over his scarred, pitted face. "When I was younger, b-back in the late fifties, I was a bouncer at a nightclub in Atlantic City, okay? Got into a-a altercation with a mean drunk who pulled a gun on me. I p-punched him in the nose just as he was getting a shot off," he said, fingering one of the bullet holes in his forehead. "I recovered, except f-for this d-damned stammer. He didn't. Hit his head on the bar, got some kind of b-brain injury and died. They nailed me for involuntary m-manslaughter and sentenced me to a nickel in Rahway. I served three."

Very had begun nodding his head to his own speed-metal beat. Bullets was an excruciatingly slow talker, what with his stammer, and the tempo was starting to get to him. "And then . . . ?"

"I-I moved home with my sister. Got steady work."

"As an enforcer for the Gambino mob, am I right?"

"I g-got nothing to say about that. Got sentenced t-to eight years in Sing Sing for assault and battery in the seventies. Served six. Got n-nothing to say about that either. Not without a-a lawyer."

"Fair enough. How long have you been driving for Muriel Cantrell?"

"Long time."

"What's your idea of a long time?"

"Twelve years."

Very raised his eyebrows. "That's my idea of a long time, too. Was she a nice lady?"

"Cream and sugar. Nicest lady I known in m-my whole life. Always a kind word. Never t-treated me like a b-big dumb gorilla. I c-can't believe she's gone . . ." His eyes moistened. "Sure will miss her."

Lulu moseyed over and sniffed delicately at the cuffs of his pants. Bullets smiled faintly at her. "Nice dog. I like d-dogs. She belong to you?"

"Actually, it's more like I belong to her."

Lulu seemed to get nothing but a positive read from the big galoot. Climbed up onto the sofa and joined him. When he petted her and told her she was a good girl, she curled up in his huge lap and stayed there, tail thumping.

Bullets let out something that sounded vaguely like a chuckle. "Sweetie, ain't she?"

"She wants to cheer you up. She can tell that you're sad."

His face fell. "It's t-true, I am," he said as he continued to pet her.

"Who hired you to drive for Muriel?" Very asked.

"Her Jew lawyer."

"Jewish lawyer, you mean?" I asked him.

He ignored me. "Panisch. Max Panisch. He was h-her lawyer for ages and ages. Died maybe six, seven y-years ago. His son, Sandy, joined up with h-him after he got out of law school. He runs the p-practice now. Same office in the same building. It's on Seventh Avenue and West Fifty-Seventh. Upstairs from the p-piano showroom."

Very frowned. "Piano showroom?"

"Whole showroom filled with Steinways. On account of it's n-near Carnegie Hall, I guess."

72

"Do you know if Muriel had someone who took care of her financial affairs for her? An accountant, business manager . . . ?"

"Same guy. Sandy Panisch."

"Is that who you called just now?"

Bullets shifted uncomfortably in his seat, taking Lulu right along for the ride with him. "Maybe yes, maybe n-no."

Another blue-and-white arrived now, followed by the medical examiner and crime scene technicians. George ran the ME and techies up to the fifteenth floor in the elevator. Frank stayed on the door, ushering residents in and out, urging them to move along. Old Harvey, who was worn out after shepherding rambunctious trick-or-treaters up and down in the elevator for two hours, headed on home. There was no need for him to stay and work the overnight shift. The building would be teeming with cops all night.

"Did Panisch pay you or did Muriel?" Very asked Bullets.

"Panisch. Mailed me a check every t-two weeks."

"Did you report it to the IRS?"

"To the p-penny. I stay out of trouble, Lieutenant. C-Can't afford another fall. That's why I d-didn't squash her sister's grandson, that no-good druggie Trevor, much as I wanted to. Little weasel was always after her f-for money. Such grief he put her through. But if anything happened to him, who would you people c-come after? *Me*." He sat there, petting Lulu. "Panisch p-paid all of Muriel's bills for her. Monthly maintenance on her co-op, phone company, ConEd, cable TV . . ."

"Do you have any idea why Muriel was in the building's service stairwell tonight?"

"No, sir. No idea at all. We were supposed t-to pick up Myrna, like I told you. That's why I was waiting here."

"Muriel didn't by any chance have a gentleman friend on the fifteenth floor, did she?"

"If she did, I didn't know n-nothing about it. My job was t-to drive her, that's all."

"Where did you take her?"

"To go shopping, g-get her hair done. Wednesdays she and Myrna would g-go to a Broadway matinee or a movie together. She'd send me out to Great Neck to pick up Myrna and then d-drive her home. Didn't want her t-to have to ride the LIRR all by herself. Myrna's good people. Real regular. Not stuck up or n-nothing. She was Muriel's b-best friend from the old days."

"Which old days would those be, Bullets?"

"They went way, way back—the forties. Fridays I'd take Muriel out t-to Myrna's to play bridge with a couple of Myrna's neighbors. Widow ladies, same as Myrna."

"What did Myrna's husband do?"

"He was a real b-big shot in the garment business. Loaded like you wouldn't believe. That house of hers is a freakin' c-castle, I swear. I'd stay put in in the Silver Cloud out in the courtyard. Read the *News* and the *Post*. Sometimes take a nap. And Myrna's colored maid always—"

"Myrna's maid of color, you mean?" I asked him

Bullets didn't ignore me this time. "You some kind of a wise guy?"

"Everyone ought to be good at something."

"I d-don't like wise guys."

"I guess that means I won't be getting a Harry and David fruit sampler from you this Christmas."

Very shook his head at me. "This is so weird. Somehow, I forgot what a pain in the ass you can be."

"Really? I'm surprised. It's one of my most memorable characteristics."

He turned back to Bullets. "You were saying about Myrna's maid . . . ?"

"She'd bring me out a sandwich. Any k-kind I wanted—turkey, corned beef. A coffee, a soda. And she let me use the john in the c-cabana by the pool."

"Anywhere else you used to take Muriel?"

"The bank."

"Which bank?"

Again he ran a huge hand over his scarred, pitted face. "Uh, I-I gotta think . . ."

"Take your time."

"Let's see, there was the Citibank b-branch on West Eighty-Sixth and Broadway, the b-branch at 230 Park Avenue, and that other one on West Fifty-Third b-between Fifth and Sixth. Then there were two Chemical Bank b-branches in Brooklyn and, uh, a-a Dime Savings Bank in Queens. Forest Hills."

"She had accounts in all of those different banks?"

Bullets nodded his huge head.

"How often did she go?"

"Once every c-couple of weeks. Never the same one t-twice in a row. She had like a regular circuit she'd m-make."

"If she had an account at one Citibank branch, she wouldn't need an account at another one," I pointed out. "She must have had safety deposit boxes at them."

"I wouldn't know n-nothing about that."

"You spent a lot of years in that Silver Cloud together," Very said to him. "What did you two talk about?

"I didn't g-get paid to talk."

"So you'd just drive around in silence?"

"We'd t-talk baseball sometimes. She was a Yankee fan."

"Are you a Yankee fan, too?"

"Met fan. But with Muriel I t-talked Yankees."

"Did she ever tell you about where her money came from?"

"No, never."

"Hear any rumors?"

"Not a one."

"How long had she owned the Silver Cloud?"

"Since it was b-brand new back in '55, she told me."

"Where did she keep it?"

"A twenty-four-hour g-garage on Columbus Avenue. Real high-class place. I'm talking white g-glove treatment."

"That's where Merilee keeps the Jag," I said. "They have some major antique wheels there."

Bullets blinked at me. "You talking about the red XK150?"

"That's the one. Belongs to my ex-wife."

"Nice car. Pretty car."

"It must be pure pleasure to drive that Silver Cloud," I said.

"You b-bet. Handles like a dream." He fell into despondent silence. "Wonder what'll happen to it."

"For now, you can drive it back to the garage and call it a night," Very told him. "You're free to go. Do you usually take the subway home?"

"No, I park my own c-car there. An '87 Buick LeSabre."

"This is the part where I say don't leave town. I'll be wanting to talk to you some more."

"You d-don't have to worry about me, Lieutenant. I won't go nowhere. I don't need no more trouble, like I said. Besides, Muriel was g-good to me." His eyes moistened again. "Sure will miss her."

"I'm sorry for your loss," Very said to him.

Lulu climbed out of his lap as the big guy got up off the sofa and made his way slowly out the front door of the building to Muriel's Rolls-Royce Silver Cloud, which was parked at the foot of the awning as usual. He paused to gaze at it for a long moment before he climbed in and drove off.

"So he's mobbed up?" I asked Very.

"Hell, yeah. Bullets Durmond was an enforcer for the Gambino crime family for most of his adult life."

"I'm missing a little something here, Lieutenant. What was Muriel Cantrell's connection with the Gambino crime family?"

"That's what we have to figure out. It may take a day or two, but we'll get there." He joined Frank and George over at the reception desk. "Tell me, did Muriel have many guests?"

"Hardly any," Frank said. "Just her late sister's grandson, Trevor Ferraro. He's maybe fifteen. Came by all the time to hit her up for money. Has himself a drug problem."

"What kind of drug problem?"

"Crystal meth," I said.

"You've seen him?" he asked me.

I nodded. "He's a tweaker. Not a doubt in my mind."

"Muriel told us not to let him into her place anymore when she wasn't home," Frank said. "He stole some of her jewels."

"Did she report him?"

"Wasn't necessary. Bullets got them back for her."

"How did he manage that?" I asked.

"How do you think?" Very said to me. "He still has connections. What does this Trevor look like?"

"He's a shrimp, barely five feet tall," Frank said. "Stringy hair."

"Did you see him this evening?"

"No, I didn't." Frank looked over at George. "You?"

George shook his head.

The door behind the reception desk opened and a grim-faced Raoul joined us, giving off a faint whiff of rum.

"Do the kids in this building invite their friends over here to trick-or-treat with them?" Very asked him.

"Sure thing, Lieutenant," Raoul said. "Quite a few of them."

"So if Trevor was dressed in, say, a Barney the Dinosaur costume, he could have sneaked his way in with a group of younger kids. Waited in the stairwell to talk to Muriel until after Alan's party broke up and tried to hit her up for money. When she refused to give him any, he wrestled her pocketbook away from her and shoved her down the stairs."

"*Dressed in a Barney costume*?" I said to him. "God, the tabloids will go nuts."

Very mulled it over, his head nodding, nodding. "I'm liking him for it. In fact, Trevor sounds like our prime suspect. Any idea where he lives?" he asked Frank.

"He drifts from one East Village crack den to another, as far as I can tell. The kid's a bum. Has a real nasty mouth on him, too."

"We'll start looking for him," Very said. "And we'll find him—especially if he has money in his pocket now."

A cab pulled up out front. Raoul hustled outside to pay the fare and escort Muriel's cleaning girl, Rosalita, in the front door. And I do mean girl. She was sixteen—eighteen tops—slim and pretty with large brown eyes and shiny black hair.

Definitely one of Raoul's yum-yums.

Definitely frightened.

"You're not in any trouble, Rosalita," Raoul assured her as she looked at him apprehensively. "But someone attacked Muriel and the police want to know if they took anything from her apartment. You've spent a lot of time there. You can tell them if anything's missing, can't you?"

"I think so," she said softly. "I mean, maybe."

"Let's go take a look," Very said.

Lulu and I joined Very as we rode the elevator up to the sixteenth floor with Raoul and Rosalita, who wore a down vest, sweater, and jeans. When we arrived at apartment 16D, we found a patrolman standing guard there. Very paused to examine whether the lock had been tampered with. It didn't appear to have been. He asked Raoul for his key and used it to open the door. A small table lamp was on. Very put on a latex glove and turned on the ceiling light, then went around turning on the kitchen and bedroom lights.

Muriel's apartment was very tastefully appointed. The living room had a dark brown velvet sofa and two matching armchairs set before a big-screen television set. She watched a lot of TV, apparently. There were copies of *TV Guide* and *Soap Opera Digest* on the glass coffee table. Candice Bergen, the star of *Murphy Brown*, was on the cover of *TV Guide* that week. Please don't ask me who was on the cover of *Soap Opera Digest*. I don't recognize any of those people. Muriel had collected lithographs of New York street scenes from the 1930s and 1940s. Very fine ones, beautifully framed. Her living room walls were lined with them. So were the walls of her small dining room. Clearly, she had loved the city of that era.

As Lulu began to carefully sniff her way around the living room, Rosalita wasted no time scurrying straight for Muriel's bedroom to have a look in her closet.

"Whoa, hang on—I don't want you to touch anything," Very called out as followed her into the bedroom, which was plush bordering on frilly. He opened the closet door for her with his gloved hand.

Muriel had loved her Chanel suits. The closet was lined with them in every color imaginable. She'd also loved shoes. Must have had a hundred pairs.

"She had three fur coats," Rosalita informed him. "Such beautiful ones. They're all still here." Then she made her way over to the jewelry box on Muriel's dressing table and motioned for Very to open it. When he did, she examined the contents carefully. Necklaces, bracelets, rings, several wristwatches. "Her best pieces are still here, I think. But I cannot be positive."

"That's okay, you're doing great," Very assured her. "Anywhere else you want to look?"

"Her Cheerios."

"I'm sorry, her *what*?"

She led him into the kitchen and motioned impatiently for him to open a cupboard over the sink and remove the box of Cheerios that was in there along with boxes of Grape-Nuts, All-Bran, and Wheaties. Muriel had liked her cereal, apparently.

"Open it," she said to him. "And stick your hand down inside."

Very glanced at me, slightly bewildered, before he opened the Cheerios box and plunged his hand in. He froze for a moment, his eyes widening slightly, before he pulled out first one, then two, bound stacks of crisp hundred-dollar bills. Each had a mustard-colored paper bank strap around it that was stamped "$10,000."

Rosalita nodded with satisfaction. "Is all here."

Very looked at her in amazement. "How did you . . . ?"

"She tol' me about it in case I ever needed to buy toilet bowl cleaner or whatever."

"Twenty thou would certainly buy you plenty of toilet bowl cleaner." He turned to me and said, "Okay, this is getting weird."

"Very," I agreed.

"Yeah, what is it, dude?"

"It's getting very weird."

"You got that right. Who *was* this lady?"

"I have no idea," I confessed. "But I sure am anxious to find out."

"Seal this apartment," he ordered the patrolman. "I want the crime scene people to do a thorough top-to-bottom search in the morning. God knows what else we'll find stashed in here."

"Right, Loo."

He thanked Rosalita before he sent her down in the elevator with Raoul, staying there on the sixteenth floor with Lulu and me as we headed back toward Merilee's apartment. It was getting late. I was bushed, plus I hadn't eaten any dinner.

"Got any plans for tomorrow?" Very asked me.

"It's Monday. Up at dawn. Put on the espresso and the Ramones. Hit the typewriter. Why do you . . . ?"

"I'm driving out to Great Neck. I'll pick you up at nine sharp."

"Why do you need me?" On Lulu's cough I added, "Us, I mean."

"Because Bullets said Myrna Waldman lives in a castle. You know how to talk to rich people. I don't. You hear things I don't, see things I don't. You'd be doing me a huge favor. Just come with me, will you?"

"Okay, but only on two conditions. One, we take the Jag. Your bucket of bolts doesn't have even the slightest acquaintance with shock absorbers, springs, struts, tie rods, proper wheel alignment. The last time I rode in it, I had a backache for two weeks. Plus I chipped a tooth when you went spelunking through that pothole on Broadway and West Seventy-Second at fifty miles an hour."

"Fine, you can drive. What's the other condition?"

"That you won't chew my ear off the whole way out there about Norma. Deal?"

"Deal."

"Want to know the greatest thing about Norma? I've never met a woman who's so totally self-reliant."

"Which, I take it, means a lot to you," I said as I steered the Jag down Lexington toward the Queens Midtown Tunnel. It was sunny and brisk out, being the first day of November, but I had the top down nonetheless with the windows rolled up so we could hear each other talk. I wore the gray cheviot tweed suit from Strickland & Sons with a cream-colored Italian flannel shirt, burgundy knit tie, and kid leather ankle boots. Very wore what he always wore—a black T-shirt under his black leather jacket, and tight jeans. Lulu rode happily in his lap, her tail thumping. She loves riding with Very. It means we're on a case.

"Dude, it's crucial. I've got a whacked-out job, not to mention my own nutsiness. I need a woman who's wrapped up in her own thing. Norma doesn't *need* me. It's a totally nontraditional relationship."

"So, bottom line, you were lying to me last night."

"Who, me? About what?"

"You *are* planning to chew my ear off the whole way to Great Neck about her."

"Cut a brother some slack, will you? I don't have anyone else to talk to about her. The dudes on the job won't talk about anything that remotely has to do with *feelings*. Besides, I'm starved for intelligent guy talk. "

"This is your idea of intelligent guy talk?"

"So what's the deal—are you going to annoy me the whole way out there?"

"Haven't decided yet." I cut over to Second Avenue at East Forty-Eighth Street and steered down to East Thirty-Sixth, where I wound us toward the entrance to the dimly lit tunnel *underneath* the East River. Trust me, it helps to not think about that. "But I do feel I should point out to you that Norma and I have a professional relationship. She's my editor. I don't necessarily want to know any details about her personal life. It's inappropriate. Also icky."

Very looked at me pleadingly.

I let out a sigh of resignation. "Okay, fine. If you want to do this, we'll do this. Merilee's the same way. Involved in her own career. Not dependent on me."

"And you two have made it work, right?"

"Aside from the part where we didn't speak to each other for ten years? We're doing great. And, by the way, there is no such thing as a traditional relationship. That's a myth, like Bigfoot and trickle-down economics."

We emerged back into the sunlight in Queens and I got onto the Long Island Expressway, popularly known as the L.I.E. The morning outbound traffic wasn't bad at all, which gave us a chance to savor some of the outer borough's notable landmarks, such as the giant red-and-white-striped Elmhurst gas tanks and Flushing Meadows, site of the 1964 World's Fair, where the Unisphere, a twelve-story stainless steel globe, still remained. Beyond that, the traffic thinned out and we started seeing green things such as trees. We crossed over from Queens into Nassau County—which is to say Long Island—at Douglaston, which produced John McEnroe, the obnoxious tennis brat, and still has a lot to answer for, as far as I'm concerned.

"I got the preliminary results from the medical examiner on Muriel," Very finally got around to mentioning. "She had no abrasions or bruises on her knees or thighs."

"Meaning . . . ?"

"Meaning she was shoved so hard from the top of the sixteenth-floor stairs that she practically did a swan dive before she hit that fifteenth-floor landing. She suffered displaced fractures to her top three cervical vertebrae, as I suspected. Death was instantaneous." He pulled his notepad from his jacket pocket and glanced at it. "In addition to her cheekbone, she also had shattered elbows, wrists, hands, and fingers. She was a fragile little lady."

"Was there any sign of a struggle?"

"The only thing that he could find was a faint redness around her right upper arm. My guess? Someone was waiting in the corridor for her when she left Alan Levin's party, grabbed her by the arm, and pulled her into the stairwell."

"Could the ME tell anything about the size of that someone's hand? Or how strong or tall he was?"

"Afraid not. It was just a faint redness, like I said. Nothing distinct."

"I'm sure you get asked this all of the time, but do you think a dinosaur could have done it?"

"I take it you mean Trevor the tweaker, dressed in a Barney costume."

"Correct."

"Do those Barney costumes have hands?"

"Of a sort."

"Then he's a definite suspect, you bet. Grabbed her pocketbook filled with cash and took off."

"How would he have gotten away?"

"Easily. He could have taken the stairs down to the fourteenth floor and caught the elevator there." Very leafed through his notepad some more. "I ran a criminal background check on Bullets Durmond. He took those two falls just like he told us. And a pal of mine on the Organized Crime Control Bureau told me the big guy was definitely an enforcer for the Gambino family. They're positive he's personally responsible for rubbing out eight rival gang members. Those are just the ones they know about. By the time Bullets turned fifty, he was getting to be too heavy and slow to be of much use to them. But he'd been a good, reliable soldier who'd served his two stints and kept his mouth shut. So they gave him a brass knuckle handshake. Put him in touch with Muriel's lawyer, Max Panisch, and got him the job as her chauffeur. Max died in '86 and was succeeded by his son, Sandy, just like Bullets told us."

"How much do you know about Sandy?"

"Not as much as I'd like to, but we have an appointment to see him later. If you still want to pursue this with me, that is."

"Try and stop me," I said as we neared Great Neck. "Which exit do I want?"

"Hang on a sec . . ." he said, grappling with the fold-up AAA road map.

Great Neck is one of the oldest and classiest of the Long Island burbs. But it wasn't until we got there and I needed concrete directions to Myrna Waldman's castle that I discovered something about Romaine Very that I'd never known before—the man didn't know how to read a map. Although, in fairness to him, it's not the easiest thing to do when you're zipping along at sixty-five miles per hour in a ragtop with a basset hound mouth-breathing in your lap.

"Um, hello, where do I get off?"

"I'm looking, will ya?" he answered irritably as he continued wrestling with it.

"I don't mean to rush you, Lieutenant, but if you don't give me an answer very soon, as in *now*, we're going to end up in Ronkonkoma."

"Okay, okay, I got it. In another mile you get off at Lakeville Road. I think."

"You *think*?"

"It looks like it'll get us there."

"You're not filling me with confidence."

"Myrna lives on King's Neck Road, and the Lakeville Road exit will get us there," he said, stabbing at the map with his finger. "We want this peninsula north of the expressway, see?"

"I can look at the map or I can drive. I can't do both."

"So get off at Lakeville Road, will you?"

So I got off at Lakeville Road, which became South Middle Neck Road even though we were heading north, not south, then became just plain Middle Neck Road. It was a commercial district, quite affluent.

Very said, "Okay, slow down . . . you want to stop here. No, wait, it's the next intersection. Check that, it's *this* one right here. Redbrook Road."

"Sure about that, Lieutenant?"

"Just shut up and hang a left."

I made a left at Redbrook Road, where the houses dated back to the 1920s, were set way back from the road, and were very impressive. It circled its way around a vast green park—Kings Point Park, according to the signage—and eventually led us to Kings Point Road, where Very told me to make a right.

The houses on Kings Point Road were, well, not exactly houses. They were more like royal country estates.

Myrna Waldman lived in a vast Tudor-style stone castle built around a cobblestone courtyard. There was a swimming pool. There was a tennis court. There were acres of emerald-green lawn that tumbled down to Manhasset Bay. The waterfront views weren't terrible. Since it was a clear, windswept day, I could actually make out the twin towers of the World Trade Center way off in the distance.

I pulled into the courtyard and shut off the engine. We got out, stretching our legs. Lulu roamed about, sniffing at all the new smells with keen, busy-nosed interest.

"Impressive little rock pile," Very observed, gazing around. "I mean, if you're into the whole waterfront-castle thing. Me, I can feel the onset of a panic attack if I'm away from the city for more than two hours."

"This surprises me. You're usually so laid back."

"Will you remind me again why I invited you?" he wondered as he rang the bell.

Myrna's maid, a thickly built black woman in her fifties dressed in a starched white uniform, answered the door.

"Good morning, I'm Lieutenant Romaine Very of the NYPD to see Mrs. Waldman."

"Yes, sir, she's expecting you. Please come in."

We came on in. Her eyes narrowed slightly when she caught sight of Lulu, but she said nothing.

Honestly? The entry hall was a major disappointment. There were no suits of armor. No stuffed heads of lions, tigers, or bears mounted on the walls. As for the two-acre living room, it had so many seating areas it reminded me of a hotel lobby. The modern décor had an interior decorator's fingerprints all over it. An interior decorator who was into bold, as in contrasting strokes of bright blue and orange, from floor to ceiling.

I heard footsteps on the pale, gray granite hallway floor, and Muriel Cantrell's best friend, Myrna Waldman, joined us. Unlike Muriel, she was long-legged and quite tall, perhaps five feet eight in her flat shoes. But like Muriel, she must have been quite a looker in her day. She still took very good care of herself. Myrna was trimly built and held herself very erect for a woman in her mid-seventies. She wore her dyed, jet-black hair in a stylish shag cut and was tastefully dressed in a burgundy cashmere sweater and tan wool slacks. A Ferragamo silk scarf was knotted artfully at her throat.

She studied me with dark brown eyes that were swollen and red from crying. "Lieutenant Very . . . ?"

"That would be me, actually," he informed her. "Thank you for seeing us. I know this must be a sad day for you, Mrs. Waldman."

"Terribly. Muriel was my oldest friend. And call me Myrna, please." Her gaze returned to me. "And your partner is . . . ?"

"Make it Hoagy," I said. "And we're not exactly partners in any known sense of the word. The short one's Lulu—unless you don't like dogs, in which case she can wait in the car."

"I wouldn't think of it. I love dogs. And she's such a cutie, isn't she?" Myrna bent down to pat Lulu's head, then straightened back up with athletic ease, studying me. "You're the author, aren't you? Merilee Nash's ex."

"That's right."

"Muriel was rooting for the two of you to get back together. She adored Merilee, and was fond of you, too. Told me you weren't a phony. This was high praise indeed coming from Muriel, believe me."

"Thanks for letting me know. I was fond of her, too."

She looked at Very again, tilting her head slightly. "So what exactly happened to her? The officers who drove me home last night were excruciatingly polite but wouldn't tell me a thing."

"I'm sorry that we had to send you home that way, but Bullets was a potential witness."

"A witness to *what*? He and I spoke on the phone this morning, and the big ape was sobbing and stammering so much that I could barely make out what he was saying. She . . . fell down a flight of stairs?"

"Not exactly," Very replied. "She was pushed. I'm sorry to have to tell you that this a homicide investigation."

Myrna's eyes widened in horror. "There must be some kind of mistake."

"No mistake, ma'am."

"But who on earth would want to *kill* Muriel?"

"It's my job to find out. That's why we're here. I was hoping we could talk a bit about her."

"Of course. Absolutely. Let's sit in the day room. Anita just built a fire in there." Myrna led us down a wide corridor past a formal dining room, a billiard room, a book-lined den, and a TV room that was fashioned to look like a home theater. "My children have been bugging me to sell this place ever since my husband, Paul, passed away," she said. "I've got thirteen thousand square feet here. Nine bedrooms. A full gymnasium. But it's my home. I don't want to live in a condo somewhere like an old lady who's counting the days until she dies."

"What kind of work did your husband do?"

"He was a rather prominent figure in the garment business. The import-export end of things. We bought this place back in the 1960s. Added on to it a couple of times. Raised the kids here. Now they're all married and I'm a grandmother and Paul's gone." She smiled sadly. "Prepare yourselves, boys, because it's amazing how fast it happens."

The day room was a cozy den at the end of the corridor. A chintz sofa and matching armchairs were grouped around a square glass coffee table that was heaped with magazines. A fire crackled in the stone fireplace. And the view of the bay out of the wraparound windows was spectacular. I suspected that this was the room Myrna used the most. She settled onto the sofa, maintaining her excellent posture. Not so much as a trace of a slump. Very and I took the armchairs.

Anita brought us a tray with mugs of steaming coffee and a plate of cookies, set it on the coffee table, and bustled out.

"Do help yourselves," Myrna said.

While we were busy helping ourselves, Lulu climbed onto the sofa and put her head in Myrna's lap.

"You don't mind, do you?" I asked.

"Not in the least," she said, scrunching Lulu's chin. "I love dogs. I miss my Jack Russell, Eddie. He was my best buddy. Are you going to be my buddy, Lulu?"

Lulu responded by lifting her head and licking Myrna's face.

Myrna let out a delighted laugh before she said, "Say, her breath is . . ."

"She has unusual eating habits. If you really want her to be your buddy, ask Anita to bring her a small plate of anchovies. Chilled, if possible."

"You're serious? This isn't some form of dry New York City wit?"

"Totally serious."

Myrna called out to Anita and ordered up a small plate of anchovies. Chilled, if possible. Anita raised her eyebrows but said nothing. Went and got it and set it on the coffee table before she put another log on the fire, poked at it, and left us.

Lulu nosed at the plate with intense interest but minded her manners.

"Is she waiting for me to feed them to her?" Myrna asked me.

"She is. Just be careful or you'll lose a finger."

Myrna proceeded to feed them to her, one by one, her face warming with fond delight. "A basset hound that loves anchovies. She's certainly an odd one. Any other quirks I should know about?"

"She's highly allergic to alcohol-based perfumes. Sneezes her head off."

"So I take it that Merilee Nash doesn't wear any."

"Never."

"What does she . . . ?"

"Crabtree and Evelyn avocado oil soap."

"Sounds divine. I'll have to try it. Paul didn't care for perfume, so I never wore it. Still don't."

"Neither did Muriel, I noticed. Just a bit of lilac powder."

Myrna nodded. "Albert was just like Paul. Couldn't stand perfume."

Albert.

"Muriel and I shared a sofa at Alan Levin's Halloween party just moments before she was murdered," I said. "She was a delightful lady, but extremely private. She never, ever talked about her past."

"She was my best friend for almost fifty years," Myrna recalled sadly. "We talked on the phone every single day. We went through . . . we went through a lot together."

"Do you have any idea who might have wanted to push Muriel down those stairs?" Very asked her.

Myrna's mouth tightened ever so slightly as she gazed out the window at a flock of seagulls that was swooping low over the windswept bay. "I do know that she was having trouble with her sister's grandson, a teenaged druggie named Trevor Ferraro. He was always after her for money. She tried to do what she could for him. Was hoping to get him into a rehab program. But the kid's a no-good bum who stole from her. I . . . I truly can't think of anyone else offhand."

Very sipped his coffee, studying her carefully over the rim of his mug. "What can you tell us about the source of Muriel's wealth? She had a chauffeur-driven '55 Silver Cloud, the most beautiful vintage Rolls-Royce on the road. She appears to have had cash stashed in safety deposit boxes all over the city. Hell, we found twenty-thousand dollars stuffed in a Cheerios box in her kitchen last night."

Myrna's face turned to stone. "You'll have to talk to her lawyer, Sandy Panisch, about that."

"Why?"

"Because you're not going to talk to me about it. She was my best friend, and let's just leave it at that, shall we?"

Very thumbed his chin. "Okay . . ."

"After Paul died, I wanted her to move out here with me. She wouldn't do it. She loved being in the city. I said, 'Bullets can come get you and take you into the city any time you want.' And she said, 'I don't want to spend the rest of my life on the L.I.E.' She wouldn't leave that apartment. It was her home. Same as this place is my home. But we saw each other a lot. Wednesdays we'd try to catch a matinee on Broadway. I love musicals. I was a chorus dancer in my youth, you know."

"So that explains it," I said.

Myrna peered at me. "Explains what?"

"There's a gracefulness to the way that you walk and move."

"Why, Hoagy, are you making a pass at me?"

"Trying to, but I don't think I'm getting very far."

She let out a laugh. "Don't let that discourage you."

"Not to worry. It won't."

She sipped her coffee, turning serious. "I broke a small bone in my foot one day in rehearsal. I just landed funny and it snapped. After it healed, I went back to work, but the same thing happened again. These days they probably could have repaired it with a pin or screw or whatever they do. But back in the forties, there was no such thing as sophisticated orthopedic surgery. My doctor simply advised me to look for a new line of work. I bounced around a bit before I ended up becoming a cigarette girl at the swankiest nightclub in town, the Copa. This was back in '44. The war was still on, but there was still plenty of night life," she recalled. "Cigarette girls were before your time, I imagine. They were a staple in high-class nightclubs. You had to wear a skirt that was so short it practically came up to your belly button, and you had to have a pair of long, shapely legs. I had them. They were my best asset. My moneymakers, I called them. Muriel and I met when she got a job there as a hatcheck girl. I was a couple of years older and wiser than she was, so I became like an older sister to her. She was a bit of a babe in the woods. But, believe me, with those blue eyes and curvy little figure, she was the cutest thing you ever saw."

"What had she been doing before that?" Very asked.

"Working behind the cosmetics counter at B. Altman," Myrna replied as she stroked Lulu gently in her lap. "But she was bored there. Didn't meet any interesting men. She wanted to meet a man. Before that she'd been a cashier in a coffee shop in Albany. That's where she was from. Her dad owned a hardware store there. Her high school sweetheart, who was a plumber, wanted to marry her. But she wanted more out of life. So when she was twenty-one she moved to New York City, got a room in a boarding house, and was hired as a Christmas temp at B. Altman. They liked her enough to offer her a full-time job. Then a customer who worked at the Copa came in one day and told her that with her looks she ought to stop by and ask for a job. So she did. And she was some kind of popular there, let me tell you. Made a fortune in tips. Plenty of high rollers asked her out, too. But Muriel wasn't interested. She was waiting for someone special. And one night, well, *he* walked in."

"*He* being . . . Albert?" I asked.

Myrna nodded her head. "Albert was the great love of her life, even though they were only together for ten years. He was such a powerful and charismatic man. He was also a married man in his forties with a wife and four children in Fort Lee, New Jersey. But he took one look into Muriel's big blue eyes, and she looked back at him, and both of their lives changed forever. It was true love, just like out of a storybook, all except for the part about him being married and Catholic. His wife was extremely devout, so divorce was out of the question. But keeping away from Muriel was, too, so in '47 he rented her an apartment on

Central Park West. The very same one she was still living in. The lease was in her name, but he paid the rent. He'd visit her there four, five nights a week. Make love to her. Shower her with clothes, jewels, anything she wanted. He insisted she stop working at the Copa because he didn't like the way other men looked at her, but he gave her plenty of spending money. He even made arrangements so she'd be well set just in case she was tempted to marry someone else for the financial security. Not that she ever would have. My God, how she loved that man. He was always buying her extravagant gifts, like that Rolls. And taking her to places like Miami, Havana, Vegas. She was his girl. And he was her guy . . ." Myrna trailed off, her face darkening. "Right up until the day he was assassinated in the barber shop of the Park Sheraton Hotel. He was fifty-five years old."

The day room fell silent aside from the crackle of the fire and the sound of Lulu snoring contentedly in Myrna's lap.

Very raised his chin at her, his eyes narrowing to slits. "Myrna, are you telling us that Muriel's *Albert* was Albert Anastasia, the founder of Murder, Inc., boss of the Gambino crime family, and the most ruthless organized crime figure in the history of New York?"

She nodded her head ever so slightly, swallowing. "He wasn't like that when he was with Muriel. She brought out the good in Albert. He was always a perfect gentleman. And when I married Paul, he gave us a lovely wedding dinner. He also did Paul a huge favor."

"What kind of a favor?"

"Albert controlled the dockworkers' union, which meant that nothing went in or out of the waterfront without his say so. He put Paul in touch with some people who were able to help him with his fledgling import-export business. I'm not naïve, Lieutenant. I'm aware that the garment business has always had links to organized crime. But Paul was no gangster. He was a reputable businessman. Albert simply did him some favors early on because we were Muriel's friends. And he never asked Paul for anything in return."

"You're sure about that, are you?"

"Positive," she snapped.

"Fair enough, but answer me this. Do you think you'd be living here in this castle if he *hadn't* done Paul those favors?"

"My understanding is that you drove out here to talk about Muriel," Myrna fired back, her nostrils flaring.

"Okay, so let's talk about Muriel," he said easily.

"After Albert was shot, I didn't think she'd make it. She wept and she wept. 'There's a hole in my heart that'll never go away,' she kept telling me. She was still a very attractive young woman. Thirty-five years old. She could have met a nice guy and gotten married, had kids even. But she never so much as looked at another man." Myrna turned her gaze on me. "Muriel and I grew up in a different era than you young fellows. First there was the Depression, then the war. All that anybody was trying to do was survive. If a show that I was dancing in folded, I'd wait tables and sling drinks to get by. Sometimes I'd go out on dates with men who gave me gifts afterward. Did that make me a call girl? Muriel was involved with a married gangster. Did that make her a floozie? Life isn't that simple. Not when it's *your* life."

"So what did she do after Albert was murdered?" I asked.

Myrna looked at me blankly. "Do?"

"Did she go back to work or travel or . . . ?"

"No, nothing like that. She stayed home, ate cottage cheese with canned peaches, and watched TV. She loved her soap operas. And she loved the old black-and-white pictures with Barbara Stanwyck and Bette Davis. I swear, she must have seen *Now, Voyager* a hundred times. Mostly, she kept to herself in that apartment and mourned. It must have been a year before she started venturing out and developing a routine. She'd go shoe shopping, get her hair done, stop by to visit her lawyer. After Paul died, the two of us would try to see each other a couple of times a week, like I said. Catch a show, play bridge. She wasn't much of a bridge player, to tell you the truth. But she was a hell of a friend." Myrna's eyes puddled with tears. "Best friend I ever had."

"I'm sorry if we've upset you," Very said.

"You haven't. I just want you to catch whoever did that to her."

"Consider it done."

"And if I can be of any further help . . ."

"You've been a huge help."

She hesitated. "Still, I'm concerned that I may not have given you as complete a picture of Muriel as I should. She was a kind and loving person, but she wasn't entirely sunshine and lollipops. She could be riled. And if you riled her, you did not want to suffer the consequences."

Very leaned forward in his chair. "Are you speaking about anyone in particular?

"Well, I do happen to know that she didn't care for that Park Avenue debutante who lived on her floor."

"Do you mean Olivia Pennington Kates?" I asked.

Myrna nodded. "That's the one. Muriel really had it in for her."

"Why?"

"Because Olivia was having an affair with another one of her neighbors, Alan Levin, and broke up his relationship with a very nice girl named Gretchen Meyer, who could have done his career a lot of good. Muriel told me that the spoiled bitch didn't even care one bit about Alan. She just liked to toy with other people's lives because she could."

Very eyed Myrna carefully. "Are you going somewhere with this?"

"I am. If Muriel had it in for a person, she'd go out of her way to hit them where it hurts. And I, well . . . I helped her."

"Helped her how, Myrna?"

"I called an old, old business associate of Paul's who he'd met through Albert and asked him to give Muriel's lawyer, Sandy Panisch, a call."

"In reference to . . . ?"

"I imagine it had something to do with Olivia's clothing line. I don't know any of the details. I didn't ask, and Muriel didn't tell. I simply did her that small favor."

"What's the name of this old business associate who you called?"

"I'd rather not say."

"I can compel you."

Myrna shrugged. "So compel me."

He stared at her for a long moment before he decided to let it go. For now, anyhow. "Thank you for sharing that with us."

"I thought you should know. It might not mean anything."

"Then again it might," he said, glancing at his watch. "And thank you for your time. We have to be getting back to the city now. Have a full day ahead of us."

Myrna roused Lulu, who yawned and climbed down from her lap. Then Muriel Cantrell's best friend stood up and led us down the long marble corridor past the home theater, book-lined den, billiard room, and dining room toward the front door. "You'll be speaking with Sandy Panisch, I imagine."

Very nodded. "Yes, we will."

"I hope he can help you. But if you want my personal opinion, this had nothing to do with Albert or any of his cohorts or enemies. Those men are long gone, and their scores were settled ages ago. Joey Gallo, who everyone said was responsible for setting up the hit on Albert at the Park Sheraton, was gunned down at Umbertos Clam House more than twenty years ago. If I were you, I'd be looking for that little druggie Trevor."

"We are, trust me. Thank you again for your time."

"Yes, thank you," I said.

She opened the door and ushered us out. "If you have any more questions, don't hesitate to call."

"Will do," Very said.

She stood there in the courtyard and watched us get back into the Jag, Lulu settling herself into Very's lap. Then she waved goodbye and went back inside her castle.

I started to put the key in the ignition, then stopped.

Very peered at me, his brow furrowing. "Something bothering you, dude?"

"Most definitely," I said, starting up the Jag with a roar.

"What is it?"

"I feel as if I've been a step slow—which is to say clueless."

"In regards to what?"

I circled the Jag around in the courtyard, pulled back onto Kings Point Road and started back the way we came. Or at least I hoped I did. "In regards to what, or make that whom, we're dealing with."

"Which is . . . ?"

"Two elderly women who spent a lot of years associating with men for whom violence was a way of life. Muriel was never who she appeared to be, and neither is Myrna."

"No one is," he said, his jaw muscles going to work on a fresh piece of bubble gum. "That was one of the first really important lessons I learned on this job. Want to know who taught it to me?"

"Who?"

He grinned at me. "You did."

CHAPTER FIVE

I t turned out that the offices of Panisch and Panisch, Attorneys-at-Law, were actually two doors down West Fifty-Seventh Street from the building that had the Steinway showroom in it, not directly upstairs as Bullets had told us. But Very and I agreed that we wouldn't hold it against the big guy.

A glamorous office building it was not. It had a narrow, dimly lit lobby and no reception desk. Just an office directory on the wall, which seemed to be packed mostly with dentists, certified public accountants, and insurance agents. Panisch and Panisch was on the tenth floor.

We rode the elevator up. It was just past one o'clock by then. It had taken us nearly an hour longer getting back to the city than I'd expected. First, we'd lost twenty minutes circling round and round in Great Neck due to Very's crack map-reading skills. On the plus side, while we were lost, we stumbled upon a fragrant family-owned Italian deli where we'd stopped to scarf up meatball heroes. Lulu had a tuna sub minus the sub. She loves Italian tuna, which is packed in olive oil instead of spring water, whatever the hell that is.

Panisch and Panisch, Attorneys-at-Law, was not exactly a white-shoe law firm. There was a sparsely furnished outer office where a gaunt, elderly secretary was pecking away at an IBM Selectric. Her eyes were red, and a damp tissue was tucked into the wristband of her sweater. There was one office with its door closed and another with its door opened that was crammed with filing cabinets.

She glanced up at us, then down at Lulu before she said, "May I help you?"

"Need to speak to Mr. Panisch, please," Very said.

She made an elaborate show of consulting her desk calendar. "I'm afraid he's rather busy. Did you have an appointment?"

He held out his shield. "I'm Detective Lieutenant Romaine Very. I'm here about Muriel Cantrell's death."

Her eyes widened. "Oh, my, of course. Just a moment please, Lieutenant." She got up, tapped on Sandy Panisch's door, and went inside. When she came back out, closing the door behind her, she said, "He'll be right with you."

Sandy Panisch had a mournful look on his face when he emerged from his office, buttoning the jacket of his suit—a charcoal-gray polyester blend with the trademark schlumpy fit that shouted SYMS, the discount clothing chain that advertised on local TV day and night. Panisch was in his fifties, pudgy and bald, with a round, pink, kindly face. He looked more like a high school social studies teacher than a mobbed-up attorney. "Come in, gentlemen," he said in a somber voice. "Please."

"Thank you, Mr. Panisch," Very said.

"Call me Sandy. Everybody does."

"Sandy, this is my associate Stewart Hoag."

"Are you with the NYPD, too?"

"In an advisory capacity," Very answered for me. "He was Muriel's neighbor."

"Is that right? And who might *this* be?" Sandy asked, bending down with a slight *oof* to pat Lulu, who sniffed delicately at the cuff of his pants and didn't let out a sound, meaning she didn't recognize his scent.

"This would be Lulu," I said. "The brains of the outfit."

Sandy said, "Miss Maimes, do we still have that box of Milk-Bones around from old man Hammermasch's schnauzer?"

"I can look around," she answered with a distinct lack of enthusiasm.

"Not necessary," I assured her. "Lulu never touches doggie treats. She has intensely strong feelings on the subject."

Sandy's office was not showy. It's hard to pull off showy when your window overlooks a grimy airshaft. The desk was good, solid oak that looked as if it had been around a lot of years, as did the two chairs that were set before it. Very and I sat in them, Lulu stretching out on the worn carpet between us. There were filing cabinets against one wall, and another wall that was filled with shelves of law books. Sandy took a seat behind his desk. He had a modest desk chair, not one of those fancy, high-backed black leather numbers that are favored by dick swingers. On his desk there was a picture of his pudgy wife and three pudgy adult kids.

If you didn't know better, you'd swear that everything about Sandy Panisch, Esq., cried out small time. Except Very and I both knew better.

"Pop never believed in wasting money on a flashy front," he explained as he noticed us looking around. "We were partners until he passed away eight years ago."

"Hence Panisch and Panisch?" I asked.

"Hence Panisch and Panisch," he acknowledged. "He got his law degree at Fordham by working nights there as a custodian. Saved his money. Never spent a nickel on fancy clothes or cars. It was his greatest dream in life that I'd go to law school someday and that we'd become partners. And we did. Except I didn't go to Fordham. He put me through Columbia Law School. And my sister, who graduated from Brandeis, is married to a professor at MIT. Applied mathematics is his field, whatever that is. Do you have any idea what it is?"

"Can't help you," I said. "I get paid to write, not to think."

He frowned at me, started to formulate a response, then decided to move along. "So now Panisch and Panisch is just a one-man practice. And Pop would be proud to know that I've carried on the family tradition. I didn't move to a fancier office when he died. Didn't trade in Miss Maimes for a sexy blonde with tits out to here. I still live in the same house in White Plains that Hilda and I have lived in for twenty years. I drive a Honda Accord that has eighty thousand miles on it. Pop believed that our job was to serve our clients, not to draw attention to ourselves."

"What sort of clients do you typically serve?" Very asked him.

"Panisch and Panisch is a bread-and-butter law firm," he replied, clasping his hands on the desk before him. "I draw up wills and serve as executor of estates. I handle closings on home sales. Draft partnership agreements, small business contracts. Pop always believed in staying away from lawsuits and divorces, and so do I. Too many late-night phone calls. Too much aggravation. He never got rich, but he made a good living over the years and so have I, but . . ." Sandy trailed off, his face falling. "But you came to see me about Muriel. Terrible, her falling down the stairs that way. What was a woman her age doing in the service stairwell anyway?"

"She didn't fall, Sandy," Very said. "She was grabbed and shoved down those stairs. It was murder."

He blinked at Very in utter shock. "You know this for a fact?"

"Those are the medical examiner's preliminary findings."

Sandy ran a hand over his pudgy pink face. "Oh, dear . . ."

"You weren't visiting her last night, were you?"

"Who, me? Heck no. I was home in White Plains handing out candy to the trick-or-treaters. Besides, I never visited Muriel. Not once. She always came here." He settled back in his chair, sticking out his lower lip. "Who would want to *murder* that sweet old lady?"

"We were hoping you could help us figure that out."

"Certainly. If there's anything that I can do to help, I'm at your service."

"You were her attorney. Did you draw up her will?"

"I did. She left almost all of her assets to the American Cancer Society. Her sister, who I gather she was very close to, died of breast cancer many years ago."

"By 'her assets' would you be referring to the contents of her safety deposit boxes?" Very asked.

Sandy's eyes flickered. "So you're aware of those. Yes, the contents of her safety deposit boxes, which I would estimate to be approximately two hundred thousand dollars. Also the net proceeds of the sale of her apartment, which she bought at a low insider price of twenty-five thousand when her building went co-op in '78. It must be worth twenty times that much now, given the location, and it will have to be sold in order to settle her estate. There's also a checking account in the firm's name that was set up so that we could write her monthly expense checks. It's not a large account. Just a few thousand."

"You said 'almost' all of her assets go the American Cancer Society," I pointed out. "Who else stands to benefit?"

He smiled faintly. "She wanted to leave the Silver Cloud to Bullets Durmond, which he is free to keep or sell."

"That was a generous gesture. That Rolls is worth a fortune."

"Indeed it is."

"Does Bullets know about it?"

"I don't believe so. Not unless she told him, and that wasn't her style. Muriel was tight-lipped. And, let's see, she left her jewelry and that fabulous wardrobe of hers to her friend, Myrna Waldman. I suppose she thought that Myrna would know best what to do with it."

"How about Trevor Ferraro?" I asked. "Is he mentioned in her will?"

Sandy's face tightened. "No, he's not. And that's an intentional slight. Recent, too. She had me revise the will just a few weeks ago. Prior to that she had intended to leave him five thousand dollars. But she told me he was a no-good druggie bum who'd stolen from her and she wanted nothing more to do with him. Cut him off cold." He fell silent for a moment. "She wished to have no funeral service. Simply wanted to be cremated and to have her ashes strewn over a certain individual's grave in Green-Wood Cemetery in Brooklyn."

"By 'a certain individual' do you mean Albert Anastasia?" Very asked.

Sandy glared at him angrily. "So *that's* why you're here? To drag her name through the tabloids? I'm disappointed in you, Lieutenant. Highly disappointed."

"I'm here for the exact reason I said," Very responded calmly. "To find out who killed her. If Muriel's death has anything to with Anastasia, then I intend to pursue it. That's my job. You mentioned he's buried in Brooklyn. Is his wife buried alongside of him or is she still alive?"

"I have no idea if she's still alive," Panisch answered tightly. "After he was bumped off, I was told that she changed her name and moved to Canada with their kids. And I want to get one thing straight right away. I had nothing whatsoever to do with him. That was Pop, not me. Hell, when Anastasia was gunned down in the barbershop of the Park Sheraton, I was a sophomore at NYU. And I want to tell you something else—Pop was in no way, shape, or form a mob attorney. He didn't set killers free by bribing jurors. He didn't make shady deals with crooked politicians. He was an honest, decent guy with a one-man family law practice over a shoe store on Flatbush Avenue in Brooklyn back in those days."

Very gazed across the desk at him. "By 'those days' you mean . . . ?"

"Back in 1947, not long after V-J Day. Pop was sole supporter of his mother, so he wasn't sent overseas, although he did serve two years in the JAG Corps in Washington. Albert, as Pop called him, was looking around for an attorney with absolutely no mob connections whatsoever.

No ties to organized labor, the restaurant business, liquor business, or any facet of the entertainment world. He wanted a nice, quiet little attorney who absolutely nobody would be able to trace back to him. So he had a friend of a friend ask around, and the name that came up was Max Panisch. Pop was just a young neighborhood lawyer with a wife and two kids. I was eight. My sister was five. We lived right there in Flatbush," he recalled fondly. "I played stickball with my pals. Read comic books at the candy store. It seems like a lifetime ago, but, believe me, I can still remember every detail of the story about how Albert came into Pop's life. Pop told it to me enough times, God knows . . ." Sandy gazed up at the ceiling, summoning the memory. "He and Miss Maimes, who was a young filly just out of secretarial school, were sitting in the office one summer day. It was a hot day. Pop was in shirtsleeves. It wasn't as if he had air conditioning. A quiet day. The phone wasn't ringing. Nothing was going on. Not until these two guys came thumping up the stairs, walked in the door, and right away he knew they were trouble. Big bruisers, both of them, wearing sharkskin suits and way too much cologne and hair tonic. Plus they had bulges under the armpits of their jackets. Greaseballs, he called him. 'Are you Panisch, the lawyer?' one of them said to him. 'I am,' Pop replied. And the other one said, 'Gentleman downstairs wants to see you.' So Pop said, 'Is he handicapped?' Which they didn't take kindly to at all. 'Is that supposed to be some kind of joke?' one of them growled. Pop hurriedly said, 'No, I was wondering if you wanted me to come down because he can't climb the stairs.' And the other guy said, 'He's got no trouble with stairs. We're just checking things out.' The two of them then proceeded to look around. Not that there was much to see. It was half the size of this office. There were two doors. One was a closet, the other the lavatory. Still, they opened both of them."

"They were casing the joint," Very said.

"Exactly, Lieutenant. They were casing the joint. Then they said, 'He'll be right up,' and left, thumping their way downstairs. A moment later Pop heard someone climbing the stairs and in walked another man. This one was impeccably dressed in a navy-blue worsted-wool suit, crisp white shirt, muted tie, and a gray fedora, which he removed when he came in the door. He carried himself with an air of great authority. Pop immediately sensed he was not a man to be trifled with. He also told me he had the coldest, blackest eyes he'd ever seen in his life. 'You're Max Panisch?' he asked him. 'I am,' Pop replied. 'Max, please to ask her to leave,' he said, meaning Miss Maimes. So Pop sent her downstairs to get a cup of coffee, and it was just the two of them alone in the office. Pop sat down behind his desk and motioned for his visitor to have a seat across from him. He sat down, gazing around the office before he stared intently at Pop with those cold eyes and said, 'My name at birth in Calabria was Umberto Anastasio,' he said. 'When I came to America people start calling me Albert, not Umberto. And they changed my last name so it ends in a letter A, not O.'" Sandy paused, smiling faintly. "It was at this point, Pop told me, that he almost wet his pants, because he realized he was sitting across his desk from the most-feared mobster in New York."

"And he had no idea why?" I asked.

"None," Sandy answered me. "'You got kids, Max?' Albert asked him. 'Yes, I have two,' Pop answered. 'Me, I got four,' Albert said. 'But I got no choice. I'm Catholic. Max, I want to hire you to take care of something for me. I'll pay you twenty thousand dollars a year, in cash, for very little work.' Mind you, guys, that was a fortune in those days. More than Pop was grossing annually from his entire practice. 'What is it that you want me to do?' asked Pop, who told me he'd begun to tremble by this point. 'What I'm about to tell you,' Albert replied, 'must stay strictly between us. As far as the world is concerned, we don't know each other. You don't tell anyone. Not even your wife, understand?' When Pop said he understood, Albert said, 'Max, I want you to take care of someone for me.' Pop gulped and said, 'I'm a lawyer, not a hit man.' Albert let out a little chuckle that made the hairs on the back of Pop's neck stand on end and said, 'I think maybe you seen too many gangster movies. I mean that I want for you watch over her, understand?' Greatly relieved, Pop said, 'Who is it that you want me to watch over?' Anyhow, as you fellows have no doubt figured out by now, Albert had fallen madly in love with a young hatcheck girl at the Copa named—"

"Muriel Cantrell," I said.

"Muriel Cantrell," Sandy echoed, nodding. "He told Pop he loved this girl so much he couldn't live without her. Being Catholic, his wife would never grant him a divorce. But he couldn't keep slipping in and out of hotel rooms and borrowed apartments. So he wanted Pop to rent her a luxury apartment on a nice, classy street like Central Park West. 'You'll put the lease in her name,' he said to Pop. 'But I'll give you the cash to pay the rent every month by check through your law firm. I also want you to pay her phone bill, electric bill, doctor bills, dentist bills, anything that is usually paid for by check. Her spending money I can give her myself. Absolutely no one is to know about this, like I said. And I am not a client, understand? I want nothing on paper between us. I will pay you your fee strictly in cash.' Albert paused, looking around. 'And

121

one other thing. I want you to move your office someplace closer to the apartment that you rent for her. It'll be easier for her to stay in close contact with you. Say, West Fifty-Seventh Street, understand?' Pop said that he understood perfectly, but that if Albert refused to officially retain him as his attorney and insisted upon paying him in cash that he didn't think he could help him out. Albert's face immediately turned beet red. He wasn't accustomed to people saying no to him. 'Why not?' he demanded. Pop gulped again and explained to him that if he was the sudden beneficiary of twenty thousand dollars of new annual income, all in cash, that he would have a very hard time explaining to the IRS where the money was coming from. Albert stared at him with those cold eyes and said, 'You can't say no, Max. You already know too much.' Which Pop took to mean that those two torpedoes downstairs were going to bump him off."

"I certainly would have taken it that way," I said.

"Likewise," Very said, nodding his head.

"Which is why I've got to hand it to Pop," Sandy said. "He was one quick-witted guy. Figured out a solution right there on the spot that saved my mom from becoming a young widow. 'You misunderstand me, Albert,' he said. 'I didn't turn you down. Merely the financial arrangement you were proposing. It would be my pleasure to take you on as a pro bono client.' Albert glowered at him and said, 'What does this pro bono mean?' And Pop explained to him that quite a number of attorneys represented a small percentage of needy clients at no charge as a form of charity work. 'But I can pay you,' Albert objected. 'I am no charity case.' And Pop said to him, 'It's the only way I can do it.' Albert shook a finger at him and said, 'You crazy.' Pop said, 'No, just careful.' And Albert said, 'Okay, careful I can respect. It's a deal.' Except that there was still one other major hurdle. If Pop suddenly started making cash deposits in his law firm's checking account that were large enough to cover the rent on Muriel's luxury apartment on Central Park West and her monthly expenses, then it would attract the bank's attention, which would in turn—yet again—attract the attention of the IRS. He explained this to Albert, who said, 'Already I can tell you're a smart fella. You'll figure something out. I have confidence.'"

"And I take it that he did figure something out," Very said.

Sandy's face broke into a grin. "He did. And I still think it was fucking brilliant. He reached out to my Uncle Benny."

"And who was your Uncle Benny?"

"*Is*, actually. He's still with us. Lives in Boca Raton with Aunt Sadie. My cousin Brucie runs the business now."

"What kind of a business are we talking about?"

"Three jewelry stores in Queens and Brooklyn as well as a half dozen very profitable pawnbroking establishments. Benny was accustomed to depositing large sums of cash in the bank. People pay cash for jewelry all the time—like, for instance, a married guy who wants to buy a fancy necklace for his mistress and doesn't want his wife to know. If he writes the jeweler a check or puts it on a credit card, his wife is liable to find out about it. So he pays cash." Sandy paused for a moment, choosing his words carefully. "Pop never exactly approved of the way Uncle Benny did business. He considered him faintly sleazy. But Benny was family, which meant a lot more in those days than it does now. So Pop approached him in the strictest confidence with a proposition. He told him he'd just taken on a couple of new clients who dealt strictly in cash—and lots of it. 'What are they, bookies?' Benny asked him. 'The less you know the better,' Pop responded. But he explained that they wanted him to deposit big chunks of cash in the law firm's bank account for them and then to start writing checks on their behalf. He told Benny the bank would sit right up and take notice, as would the IRS, but they wouldn't if he, Benny, with his jewelry stores and pawnshops, became a client, deposited their cash in his own account, and wrote the law firm a check for that amount every month for various legal services rendered. Laundered it for him, in other words. Benny, who'd always thought that Pop was strictly a goody two-shoes, was happy to help. Thrilled, even. He was tickled to see him mixed up in something that smelled a bit, um . . ."

"Unsavory?" I suggested.

"Exactly. In fact, he was so tickled he refused to take any money from Pop in return. 'Family's family,' he said. So that's how Pop pulled it off. He found Muriel that apartment. Took out a lease on this office. And the rest you know."

"Is your mother still alive?" I asked.

Sandy's face fell. "No, she passed away three years ago."

"How much did she know about this?"

"Not one bit. Pop was afraid to tell her because he knew she would be furious that he'd gotten mixed up with gangsters. Hell, he didn't even tell her he was representing Uncle Benny, who she thought was a *ganef.*"

"Anastasia has been dead for thirty-six years," Very pointed out. "And yet, seemingly, the cash has never stopped flowing. Where has it been coming from?"

"A couple of different sources. Initially, it came from a pair of suitcases that Pop said those two greaseballs of Albert's delivered to this office on the very day that he got rubbed out at the Park Sheraton, both of them looking shaky, pale, and really anxious to clear out of town. 'You won't be seeing us no more,' one of them said. And out the door they went. When Pop opened the suitcases, he discovered they were stuffed with cash, five hundred thousand in all, which he immediately put in the law firm's safety deposit box in the Chemical Bank down the street. Every month he'd withdraw the usual monthly sum from the box to cover Muriel's expenses, pass it along to Uncle Benny, who'd then deposit it in the firm's account and write Pop a check for legal services rendered so that Pop could continue to write Muriel's checks." Sandy paused for a moment, reflecting. "On that warm afternoon in Flatbush back in 1947, Albert had made it clear to Pop that should anything happen to him, he still intended to take care of Muriel for the rest of her life. He truly loved her. Nothing was too good for her, like that Rolls-Royce Silver Cloud he bought her in '55. He even hired her a chauffeur to go with it. Bullets must be the fourth or fifth she's had over the years, though he's served the longest by far. Albert confided in Pop that he'd rented safety deposit boxes in a half dozen banks around the city in her name. 'I've put two hundred fifty thousand in cash in each box for her so she can live out her days comfortably and also not feel she needs to find another means of support, if you know what I mean.' Pop knew exactly what he meant."

"He didn't want another man going near his beloved Muriel," I said.

"Precisely. Albert had also made a confidential arrangement with each bank manager so that every two years the cash in the safety deposit boxes would be replaced with fresh currency so that she didn't end up sitting on a pile of antique money, which might attract attention. Banks aren't supposed to have both keys to those boxes, only one. The box holder has the other. But, as Albert put it, 'You can buy a branch manager same as you can anyone else.' And, in case you're wondering, Pop made a similar arrangement with the manager of the bank down the street to regularly refresh that half mil from those suitcases. Albert told Pop that he didn't want Muriel to know anything about her safety deposit boxes unless something happened to him. The contents were her inheritance, was how he put it. He wanted Pop to use the money to pay her monthly bills same as always as well as to provide her with spending money. Not that we needed to go near the boxes for a long, long time. The five hundred thousand in those two suitcases that the greaseballs delivered the day Albert was murdered paid her way until the early seventies. It wasn't until then that we finally told her about the safety deposit boxes Albert had left her and handed over the keys to them that he'd left with Pop for safe keeping."

127

"How did she respond?" I asked.

"She didn't," Sandy said with a curious look on his face. "Wasn't happy. Wasn't sad. She was very cool-headed about the whole matter. It was . . . very odd. All I could figure was that she must have known about them all along. She was one shrewd little lady. Mind you, it did mean there was also a slight change in procedure. Since the boxes were in her name, Muriel had to become an active participant and withdraw the cash personally, then give it to us to pass along to Uncle Benny—or, in recent years, to Cousin Brucie."

"And was that a problem for Muriel?" I asked.

"Not in the least. She loved handling cash. I mean, *loved* it."

"So we've heard," Very said. "Bullets did tell us about her regular visits to a half dozen banks scattered around the city. This explains it. She was drawing on her inheritance."

Sandy nodded. "Had been for years."

"Tell me, how often did your father meet with Albert?" Very asked.

"Just that one time, believe it or not. Pop never saw him again until he picked up the newspaper and looked at those photos of Albert lying dead on the floor of the barbershop of the Park Sheraton. Pop said that Muriel was a total wreck. Hardly left her apartment for a month. He did what he could for her, but she barely said two words to him. He contacted her good friend Myrna, but I gather Myrna didn't have much luck either. Albert was the love of her life. From that point on, she lived like a widow, even though Pop said she was still quite a youthful dish. She loved nice clothes. Loved getting her hair done and looking sharp. But, as far as Pop knew, there was never anyone else. She never even went out on a date." Sandy paused, considering his next words carefully. "Muriel was always polite to me, but our relationship was strictly business. She never confided in me. She was a private person. A solitary person. She loved that apartment. It was *their* apartment. She developed a fondness for lithographs of New York street scenes from the thirties and forties. I guess they reminded her of when she first came to town. She liked to visit the Old Print Shop on Lexington in Murray Hill. Bought quite a few from them. They're valuable in their way, but hardly extravagant for a woman of her wealth. That's the only interest she developed that I'm aware of. Mostly, she liked to sit home and watch her soaps on TV." Sandy sat back in his chair again with his hands resting on his tummy. "I joined up with Pop in '68 after I passed the bar exam, and the name of the firm officially became Panisch and Panisch, which was a dream come true for him. My first official day of work, he called me into his office, this office, and said, 'Now that we're partners, there's a little story that I have to tell you about one of our pro bono clients. And your mom must never, ever know a word know about this.' Trust me, guys, I was flabbergasted when he told me. I couldn't believe he'd been sitting on a secret like that for over twenty years. But Pop took the matter of client confidentiality seriously. And he took Muriel seriously. There was nothing flighty about her—especially when the subject was money. She would ask a lot of specific questions. Demand thorough answers. She could get very stubborn and quarrelsome. You wouldn't know it look at her, but she was one tough little broad."

"Myrna told us pretty much the same thing," Very said. "That Muriel was no cream puff, I mean."

"Indeed not," Sandy agreed, nodding his round, bald head. "Myrna's no cream puff either. Those two went through some lean times in their youth. The Depression. The War. That generation is a lot more hard-nosed than we are, in my opinion. Anyhow, I've seen to Muriel's needs ever since Pop died in '85. Once every month, she'd bring me money from one of the safety deposit boxes. I'd work the same laundering arrangement with Cousin Brucie that Pop had with Uncle Benny. I'd write her monthly checks for her, and she'd keep a generous amount of cash for herself."

"We found twenty thou in hundred-dollar bills in a Cheerios box last night," Very said.

"I'm not surprised. She found it comforting to have cash around."

"What can you tell us about this grandson of her sister's, Trevor Ferraro? Aside from the no-good, druggie-bum part."

Sandy furrowed his brow thoughtfully. "Not much. Just that he dropped out of high school and ran away from home. His parents live in Yonkers. Trevor's father, Tom, was her sister's only child."

"Did Muriel make any provisions for Tom in her will?"

"She did not. Some years back, Tom learned the details of Muriel's relationship with Albert and, I'm told, made some very unflattering remarks to her. From that moment on he was dead to her. When Trevor ran away from home the kid came looking for her. She was fond of him, at first. But then . . ."

"He turned out to be a no-good druggie bum?" I suggested.

"Exactly."

"We were told it was Bullets who managed to locate the jewelry that Trevor stole from her," Very said.

Sandy nodded. "So I heard. He still knows people. His hands aren't entirely clean. Being candid, mine aren't either. Any lawyer, no matter what kind of law he or she practices, comes in contact with people who've done something they shouldn't have—whether it's cheat on their spouse, embezzle money from their delicatessen, or stab somebody in the eyeball with an ice pick. Muriel wasn't anyone's idea of a criminal. Yet she also had no qualms whatsoever about living very comfortably for thirty-six years on piles and piles of cash that she knew perfectly well had been obtained by racketeering, murder, drug trafficking, prostitution, and God knows what else. She was the beneficiary of Albert Anastasia's criminal enterprises for half of her life. Did that make her complicit? Should Pop have been disbarred for acting on her behalf? Should I be? I don't know the answer to any of that. The world isn't that simple from my side of the desk. But I always tried to do my best for Muriel, and I grew to be fond of her over the years." He let out a sad laugh. "She always gave me a new necktie every Christmas. I'd tell my wife that it was Miss Maimes who'd given it to me, because my wife has never known a thing about my association with Muriel."

"Like father, like son?" Very asked.

"Exactly, Lieutenant. I'll miss her. I know Miss Maimes will, too. She's quite upset. And I imagine that Myrna must be devastated. She and Muriel were close friends since forever. I should give her a call, tell her how sorry I am."

"Have you spoken to her recently? Or to an associate of her husband's, perhaps?"

"Why, no. Not in ages." Sandy suddenly got busy rearranging the memos on his desk. He wasn't a very convincing liar, especially considering that he was an attorney. "Why do you ask?"

"Just curious." Very's jaw muscles went to work on a fresh piece of bubble gum. "Myrna told us that her late husband, Paul, was a powerful figure in the garment industry, particularly the import-export end of things."

"That's right. Pop told me that Albert, strictly as a favor to Muriel, gave Paul a little boost early on in his career. What with the clout Albert had on the waterfront with the dockworkers' union, he was able to make it a bit easier for Paul to do business and harder for the other firms. But Paul built his business on his own after that. He was considered a reputable guy, or as reputable as they come in the garment business. That's a nasty business. But you two don't look as if you need me to tell you anything about how nasty a world we live in."

"I'm curious about something," I said. "You mentioned that you thought that Muriel had maybe a total of two hundred thousand remaining in her safety deposit boxes.

If she hadn't been murdered last night, she might very likely have lived on for another ten or even fifteen years, correct?"

Sandy nodded. "She was in good health, as far as I know."

"Yet it sounds as if she only had enough money to support her lifestyle there for another, what, four or five years? Had you talked to her about her future? Possibly selling the Silver Cloud and letting Bullets go, for instance?"

"I tried talking to her until I was blue in the face. I thought that it was imperative that we have a plan for dealing with the future. Selling the Silver Cloud was certainly the most obvious option. It would fetch a great deal of money, and she'd no longer have to pay Bullets's salary, which would lower her overhead immensely. I also floated the idea of selling the apartment on Central Park West and moving to a slightly more modest doorman building on, say, West End Avenue. She would have netted a huge amount of money."

"And . . . ?"

"She refused to discuss it. And when I say refused, I mean she literally got up and walked right out of this office." Sandy got a faraway look on his face for a moment. "I know this may sound strange to you fellows, but to my mind Muriel was lucky she didn't have to do any of those things. She was still right where she wanted to be, in her love nest that she'd shared with Albert. And she still made it around town in her chauffeured Silver Cloud to shop for those Chanel suits of hers and get her hair done and go browsing for lithographs. She was living the life she wanted to be living."

"Is there a point to this, Counselor?" Very demanded, an impatient edge in his voice.

"Just this . . ." Sandy Panisch answered. "Whoever pushed Muriel down those stairs last night? That person actually did her a favor."

"She was a mean old bitch. I hated her. Hate, hate, hated her."

We were seated facing Central Park in the apartment of Merilee's neighbors, Gary and Olivia Pennington Kates, and it was Olivia who was doing the hate, hate, hating. But you've probably figured that out already.

Unlike Merilee's place, with its vintage Stickley furniture that seemed perfectly at home in the classic prewar building, Gary and Olivia's apartment was done up more like a modern converted Tribeca loft. The furniture was low slung with a huge emphasis on white leather, chrome, and glass. The Kates were also serious collectors of modern art. The living room featured two works by Jean-Michel Basquiat, the young black artist from Brooklyn, by way of Haiti and Puerto Rico, who'd taken the New York art world by storm in the early '80s—right up until he died of a drug overdose in 1988 at the age of twenty-seven. But Basquiat continued to be taken so seriously by art critics that the Whitney had just given him a major retrospective last year. His work was an in-your-face mash-up of street art, graffiti, felt-tip marker drawings, and collages. Some of it was aggressively grotesque. Can't say I enjoyed looking at it, but there was no denying that Basquiat had been the hottest young art talent on the New York scene in recent years—right up there with the great Julian Schnabel, who was famous for his enormous broken-ceramic-plate paintings. The Kates had one of those hanging in their living room, too. I thought Schnabel's work was pretentious crap, but this is America, and everyone has a right to his or her own taste. Or total lack thereof.

Olivia was wearing an oversized, scoop-neck white knit sweater with—trust me—absolutely nothing underneath it, and a pair of tight jeans to show off her slim, perfect figure. She was barefoot to show off her slim, perfect feet. Her toenails were painted blue. Her long, straight blonde hair was tied up in a bun to show off her long, regal neck. She was very attractive, and she knew it. Had known it ever since she was a little girl and noticed the way grown men stared at her. She was also a spoiled brat who was accustomed to getting whatever, or whomever, she wanted.

She studied Very with keen, blue-eyed interest, same as she had last night at the Halloween open house. She'd become particularly interested in his biceps as soon as he took off his leather jacket. The apartment was quite warm, no doubt so that she could walk around barefoot and show off her slim, perfect feet. "You seem awfully young to be a homicide lieutenant," she observed, her eyes gleaming at him. "How did you manage that?"

"I get results," he replied as he and I sat there on the low-slung white leather sofa, which was remarkably uncomfortable.

"No, it's more than that. You must have connections. This world is all about connections." Olivia bent down to retrieve her coffee mug from the glass coffee table in front of the sofa and gave both of us, particularly Very, a nice, unobstructed view of her perky pink nipples inside of that scoop-necked sweater. If she was hoping to get a rise out of him, as it were, she failed. His eyes didn't so much as widen a fraction of an inch.

"So why did you hate, hate, hate Muriel?" I asked her.

Olivia's blue eyes turned ice cold. "Because she messed with my business. Not only cost me a fortune but humiliated me. *Nobody* humiliates Olivia," she said, speaking of herself as a corporate entity, much like Calvin (Klein) or Ralph (Lauren), although I don't know if they referred to themselves in the third person in normal conversation. Not that this was my idea of normal conversation. "She made it impossible for me to ship any of Olivia's leather goods—by which I mean hundreds of pairs of shoes, handbags, and gloves—out of Italy and into the United States. I'm talking about merchandise that had already been presold to *the* most exclusive retailers, who'd already featured it in their fall catalogs, and Olivia couldn't deliver them. They were held up over there because of quote-unquote irregularities with my import-export license," she said angrily as she paced around the living room with her coffee cup. When she got over near the front door, where Lulu was stretched out, Lulu immediately growled at her. Olivia came to a frightened halt. "Why doesn't your dog like me?"

"Can't help you with that. She doesn't always tell me everything. What sort of quote-unquote irregularities?"

"Applications that hadn't been filled out properly, except that they *had* been. Total bullshit. Meanwhile, the merchandise is still there. It'll be there forever. I have top attorneys, both here and in Milan, but Muriel had some kind of special pull, because *nothing* left the country. That old bitch turned Olivia into a laughingstock. I'm basically out of the leather business now. She ruined me."

"Forgive me, I'm a bit confused," I said, tugging at my ear. "What makes you think that sweet old lady had anything to do with it?"

"First of all, she was *not* a sweet old lady—so just put that idea right out of your pretty little head. Second of all, she *told* me she did it."

"She *told* you she did it?" Very repeated in surprise.

"She most certainly did, while we were waiting to ride down in the elevator one day."

"When was this?" he asked her.

"During the summer, back when we were still on schedule for Olivia's fall season delivery."

"Do you remember what she said to you?"

"I can remember every word, because it was so creepy. She said, 'You think you're special. You're not. You think that nothing bad will ever happen to you. You're wrong.' And then she said, 'I wonder if you know how much I despise you.' When I asked her why, she told me she'd seen Alan coming out of my apartment that afternoon. We'd been fucking our brains out in one of the guest bedrooms, and I was hanging all over him in the doorway, wearing a silly grin and nothing else. 'I believe in Alan's talent,' Muriel said to me. 'Gretchen does, too. She's good for him. You're not. You're just toying with him because you feel entitled to toy with whomever you want. And you've always gotten away with it, haven't you? Well, not this time, missy. This time you're going to pay for what you've done.'"

Very sat there nodding his head to his own rock 'n' roll beat. "She said all of that?"

"She did," Olivia bent over to put her cup back on the coffee table, treating Very to another good look at her nipples. Again, he didn't react.

Me, I was starting to wonder if it were *she* who'd shoved Muriel down those stairs. True, Olivia had come to the Halloween party dressed as Glinda the Good Witch from *The Wizard of Oz*, and Glinda would never have done something so heinous. But this was so-called real life. "And what did you say to her when she told you this?"

"I said, 'Mind you own business, you old bitch.' And then I put it out of my mind. But when I couldn't get Olivia's leather goods out of Italy, I thought about our little conversation and was suddenly positive that she was behind it. Don't ask me how, because I can't even imagine. She was a just a little old lady who watched soap operas all day. Gary was absolutely furious about the whole thing. He has a huge ego and took it highly personally. He was positive that someone was trying to make *him* look bad, because he's supposed to be so tough, yet he couldn't do a thing to help me. He promised me he'd devote every resource at his disposal to finding out what happened, but he still hasn't been able to. Whoever did it covered their tracks really well."

Then again, maybe Gary *had* found out what happened and kept it from Olivia because he wanted to handle it in his own way. His own way being confronting Muriel in the hallway after Alan's Halloween party. His blood was already boiling after his stupid wrestling match on the carpet with Alan. Maybe *he* confronted Muriel in the hallway and demanded to know if she'd messed with Olivia's leather goods. Maybe when he didn't get the answer he wanted to hear, *he* gave her that fatal shove down the stairs.

I heard a rattling of keys out in the hall. The apartment door opened, and corporate America's reigning predator came strutting in wearing a rather gaudy chalk-striped suit and carrying a briefcase, which he flung on a chair by the door. Gary's nose was red and swollen from his scuffle with Alan. He also had a fat lip. His gaze chilled instantly when he caught sight of Very and me sitting on his sofa. "What are *you* guys doing here?" he demanded as Lulu scampered to the floor by my feet, a low growl coming from her throat. "Don't tell me Mr. Piano Man is pressing assault charges against me for protecting the sanctity of my home."

Olivia let out a cackle of laughter. "You did *not* just say that, did you?"

He glared at her in hostile silence.

"Oh my god, you did! This is too funny. I'll have to write it down so I don't forget it. Did the boys at the office say anything about your fat lip and big red nose?"

"I *don't* want to talk about it," he snarled at her. "And do you want to knock off your nasty remarks and tell me what's going on here?"

"They're trying to find out if any of the neighbors saw or heard anything last night before Muriel was shoved down those stairs."

Gary's face dropped. "Oh, I see. Sad business. She seemed like a nice old bird, not that I knew her more than to say 'Hello' to her in the elevator." He narrowed his eyes at Olivia. "What did you tell them?"

"That we didn't. See or hear anything, that is. What are you doing home so early?" she asked him. "It's barely four o'clock."

"I have to shower, shave, and change into fresh clothes. I'm taking a dozen very rich Hong Kong businessmen out for a night on the town. That means steaks at Peter Luger's followed by a whole lot of bar hopping before we end up at a high-end strip club with a VIP room. Don't wait up for me."

She raised her chin at him, hands on her narrow hips. "You're taking them to a strip club?"

"It's expected. Don't tell me you have a problem with it."

"Who, me? No problem. Nope, none at all."

"Good."

"Have you got time to answer a few questions on another subject?" Very asked him.

"Yeah, okay. But make it snappy, will you? I've got to be out of here in thirty minutes. What subject?"

"The embargo of Olivia's leather goods."

"That was somebody pulling a fast one." Gary shook his finger angrily at Very. "And people don't do that to me—or mine."

"You aren't going to start talking about the sanctity of your home again, are you?" Olivia said to him mockingly.

"It was an old-fashioned hose job, Lieutenant," Gary said, paying no attention to her. "Somebody had it in for me."

"So you're suggesting it was directed at you," I said. "Not at Olivia."

"Not suggesting it. *Saying* it. She hasn't made any enemies in the business world. I have. I've consolidated corporations, restructured them, downsized them. An unfortunate side effect is that sometimes there has to be a significant reduction of the workforce."

"In other words, people lose their jobs," I said.

He nodded. "And I'm not just talking stockroom clerks. Some of those people are big-time CEOs. People with clout. People with a grudge. The kind of people who lie awake at night dreaming of a way to get even with me. I guarantee that's why Olivia couldn't get her merchandise out of Italy. And, trust me, when I find out who's responsible, I'll make him one sorry son of a bitch. But I haven't heard so much as a whisper. People don't want to talk about it. Some of them have even hung up on me. People don't usually hang up on me."

I looked at him in surprise. "Really? I should think that would happen to you all the time."

Olivia let out another cackle of laughter.

He glared at her. "You want to shut the hell up?"

She clamped a hand over her mouth. "Yes, master. So sorry, master."

"But this isn't over yet. I've hired a top international detective agency. They've got operatives in Italy who'll get to the bottom of it. Count on it. Is there anything else?" he demanded impatiently.

"Just one thing," Very said. "Where'd you go after the Halloween party?"

"We came right back here, drank two bottles of wine, and screamed at each other for hours." He glanced at me. "I'm surprised you didn't hear us."

"The walls in this building are pretty thick."

"It was actually quite therapeutic," Olivia said. "I agreed I'd never see Alan again, and Gary agreed he'd give up Adriana, his Brazilian teenager. We apologized to each other, and then we had amazing makeup sex."

"Do we have to share the details of our private life with these two pomegranates?" Gary asked her irritably.

Lulu let out a low moan at my feet.

He scowled at her. "What's your dog's problem now?"

"She's upset that you didn't say these *three* pomegranates."

"I don't have time for this idiocy," he blustered, marching off down the hallway to shower and change clothes.

Olivia watched him go before she turned back to us and said, "So typical. He has to make what happened to Olivia's leather goods about *him*. But he's wrong. I know he's wrong. I just keep wondering if it's remotely possible that Muriel actually knew someone in Italy who could arrange to screw things up that way."

Very said, "From what I've been able to gather about her so far, it seems highly unlikely. She led a quiet life. But I'll widen out and see if she had any friends or acquaintances whom we still don't know about."

"Thank you, Lieutenant. I know it seems crazy, but she sounded so . . . so *determined* that day in the elevator. Maybe she was just resentful."

"Of what?" he asked her.

"That I'm young, rich, beautiful, and have great sex with whoever I want, and she was a shriveled up old lady with nothing to live for. I mean, let's face it—if someone hadn't pushed her down those stairs, she would have been sitting in a diaper in a nursing home somewhere in another few years. That's what happened to my Aunt Delia. The highlight of her day was sing-along hour."

Very sat there lost in thought for a moment. "When you two came home from the Halloween party, you were both here the whole time, am I right? There's no chance that one of you slipped out for a minute and shoved Muriel down the stairs?"

"No chance. I can certainly vouch for Gary. He never left this apartment."

"And I assume he'll vouch for you, too. Unless, that is, he'd lie to protect you." He raised his chin at her. "Would he?"

She had to think that one over. "I honestly can't give you an answer. I'm afraid I don't know him that well." An odd response, to be sure. But I've learned not to judge other people's marriages. My own is plenty nutty. "The only thing I can say with some degree of certainty after living with him for these past eight years is that he has absolutely no sense of personal morality whatsoever." Olivia moseyed over to the coffee table and bent over to remove one of her business cards from a tray that was there as well as—need I say it—treat Very to yet one more look at her perky pink nipples. "In case you ever want to talk again," she said, handing it to him. "And, just so you know, Gary doesn't care who I sleep with. Not at all."

"Is that right?" Very studied her curiously. "He seemed plenty pissed off about Alan last evening."

"Only because he'd been embarrassed. He hates to be embarrassed."

"You said he has no sense of personal morality whatsoever."

"That's correct."

"Do you?"

"Oh, absolutely," she assured him. "I live the way I want to live. I do what I want to do and *who* I want to do—and I couldn't care less what other people think."

Me, I sat there on that incredibly uncomfortable low-slung white leather sofa staring at Julian Schnabel's hideous broken-plates painting and thinking that Olivia Pennington Kates, Park Avenue debutante, clothing designer, magazine publisher, and all-around It Girl, had a lot more in common with Albert Anastasia than I would have guessed. The only thing that she hadn't done was kill anyone.

Unless, that is, she had.

"What can I tell you?" Alan Levin said to me as he sat there mournfully at his piano wearing a rumpled flannel shirt, baggy corduroy trousers, and the battle scars of last night's scuffle with Gary. His left eye was swollen half shut and turning a lovely shade of purple, and he had a bandage over the bloody fingernail gouge on his forehead. "I was so gaga over Olivia it was as if she'd cast a spell on me. As soon as those blue eyes of hers zeroed in on me, I was powerless to resist her."

There was still a great deal of police activity going on in the hallway outside of Alan's apartment. Crime scene technicians were continuing to examine the stairwell banister for prints and the steps for scuff marks. Polaroid photos were being taken of every square inch.

Very had paused to talk to them for a moment before he joined me on the sofa next to the piano. Lulu was curled up on my feet, dozing.

"Have they found anything?" I asked him.

"Maybe something. Maybe nothing."

"Care to translate that?"

"The service stair door handles weren't wiped clean. Not on this floor or on the fifteenth. There are prints all over them."

"This surprises you?"

"Most definitely."

"Maybe Muriel's killer wore gloves and wasn't worried about leaving prints behind. Olivia, for instance, was showcasing her own merchandise when she showed up here in her Glinda costume. Mauve-colored kid leather gloves that came up to her elbow."

"Hoagy's right," Alan recalled. "I noticed those gloves right away because Billie Burke didn't wear any in the movie."

"Really? I didn't notice," Very said, which sounded a whole lot like he was doing a number on Alan. Because there was nothing that Romaine Very didn't notice.

Alan began softly playing Vince Guaraldi's jazzy theme song from those popular Charlie Brown specials that had been running on TV for years. "Anyhow, it's like I was saying—I lost my head. I mean, as a rule, women who look like Olivia Pennington Kates do not want to hop in bed with Fanny and Herschel Levine's son Alan. Richard Gere I'm not." He continued to play, gazing out his windows at the sun that was getting low over the Hudson in the distance. "This was Gretch's favorite song. She was always asking me to play it. She loved those Charlie Brown specials." He sighed gloomily. "Forgive me. If it sounds as if I'm wallowing in self-pity, it's only because I am. Not only did Gretch move out on me last night, but Olivia and Gary have patched things up, and she phoned me this morning and dumped me. It seems that she hates, hates, hates messes."

"For someone who hates, hates, hates messes, she sure has a knack for getting into them," I pointed out.

"I wouldn't know. All I know is that yesterday I was involved with two women, and today I'm utterly alone. It's my own damned fault, too. I lost my head over that blonde she-devil and destroyed a great relationship with a great woman. My therapist thinks I made such a poor choice because I have self-esteem issues. But do you have *any* idea what a dream come true it was to get naked with a golden goddess like that? Well, I guess you would, Hoagy, being married to a gorgeous movie star. But *you* understand, don't you, Lieutenant?"

"No, I *don't* understand," Very responded was surprising vehemence. "If you love a woman then you don't carry on with someone else behind her back. That's not a self-esteem issue. You're a cheat, that's all. Not to mention stupid."

"Very," I chimed in, nodding.

He glanced over at me. "Yeah, dude?"

"He's very stupid."

"You got that right."

Alan sat back from the keyboard, gazing out at the Hudson again. "It's true, I am. Muriel was furious with me when she heard the scuttlebutt from Rosalita. Marched right over here, pounded on my door, and demanded to know how I could let that stuck-up tramp destroy what Gretchen and I had together. 'Gretchen *loves* you!' she hollered at me. 'Gretchen *believes* in you!' Boy, she really let me have it. And I deserved every word of it, too. Blew the best thing that's ever happened to me. I'm weak. My therapist also thinks that I'm afraid I don't have the depth to pull off a Broadway musical—so I purposely sabotaged my relationship with Gretch to kill any chance that her father would consider producing it."

"That's sounds like twenty-four-karat psychobabble to me," I said. "I'd shop around for a new therapist if I were you."

Alan looked at me in dismay. "I've been seeing him three times a week for fifteen years. He's the glue who holds me together."

"Hello, getting back to Muriel if you don't mind?" Very still seemed annoyed by the guy. "Any idea who might have wanted to shove her down those stairs?"

Alan stuck his lower lip in and out. "The only person I can think of is that drugged-out nephew of hers. He was always sponging money off of her, and I hear she cut him off."

"Did Muriel ever tell you anything about where her money came from?"

"Not a word, Lieutenant. She never discussed her past. And I never pried. I just figured she came from a wealthy family, even though she didn't act like it. She was real down to earth. And nice to me. She once told me . . ." Alan's voice caught. "She told me I had greatness in me." He shook his head miserably and went back to playing the Charlie Brown theme.

Lulu stirred at my feet as someone unlocked his front door and came in.

It was Gretchen. She stood there glaring at Alan, her face clenched tight.

He looked up at her hopefully from his piano bench. "Hey, Gretch, we were just talking about you. What brings you by?"

"I forgot to give you back your keys," she said coldly.

His face fell. "Oh . . . You could have just left them at the front desk with Frank."

"Did he call you on the house phone to tell you I was coming up?"

"Who?"

"Frank."

"Why are you asking me that?"

"Because you're playing my song."

He shrugged his soft shoulders. "I've been playing it all day. I'm blue. I miss you. I don't want you to leave me."

"You should have thought of that before you started sneaking around with that bitch."

"I'm an idiot."

"Tell me something I don't already know."

"I want you to move back in. I'm on my knees, begging you." Which, in fact, he was, his hands clasped before him beseechingly.

"Will you get up off of the floor?" Gretchen said scoldingly. "You're acting like an idiot."

"Because I *am* one. I just told you."

"And your eye looks terrible," she said, softening slightly. "Have you been icing it?"

"Should I be?"

"Helpless. You're totally helpless." She marched into the kitchen to prepare an ice pack for him.

Very got up off the sofa. "We're done here. And you two need to talk."

"No, we don't," Gretchen said from the kitchen. "There's nothing to talk about."

"Sure there is." Alan was still on his knees. "Please stay a few minutes. Stay and have a glass of wine with me."

She returned from the kitchen with the ice pack. "Well, okay . . . if you insist. But put this on your eye, and will you *please* get up off your knees?"

We let ourselves out. The crime scene technicians were still at work on the stairwell.

"That was an extremely tactful exit, Lieutenant."

"Tact had squat to do with it. I was sick of listening to that unfaithful blob wallow in self-pity. You think there's a chance she'll take him back?"

"Wouldn't surprise me one bit." I glanced at grandfather's Benrus. "It's nearly five and we've put in a pretty grueling day. Care for a beer?"

"You talked me into it."

I unlocked the door to the apartment and flicked on some lights. Merilee was still at her agent's office plotting her next career move. I went into the kitchen, fetched Lulu an anchovy and Bass ales for Very and me, then joined him in the living room, where he'd flopped down on the settee. I handed him his Bass and sat in one of the armchairs. Lulu stretched out on the settee next to Very. He reached over and patted her. Dusk had fallen. Lights were coming on in the buildings across the park on Fifth Avenue in the city that never sleeps. It was my favorite time of day to gaze out of Merilee's windows.

Very took a long gulp of his Bass, sighing gratefully. "Okay, dude, lay it on me. What's on your mind that you haven't told me?"

"Why would you ask me that, Lieutenant?"

"Because you always have a bunch of genuinely whack ideas bouncing round in that brain of yours. Never fails."

"I'm not sure if that was a compliment or an insult."

"It was a hybrid."

"Okay, I can accept that." I sipped my Bass in thoughtful silence.

"Well . . . ?"

"How do we know that Myrna was in the Loews multiplex on Broadway and West Eighty-Fourth watching *Sleepless in Seattle* when someone shoved Muriel down those stairs?"

"My men picked her up there."

"But how can you be sure that she was actually inside the theater watching the movie from 6:15 until 8:30?"

"Because she'd be able to tell us what it was about in specific detail."

"Muriel told me she'd seen it five times."

"Where on earth are you going with this?"

"Bullets drops her off there in the Silver Cloud. As soon as he drives away, she am-scrays over here on foot. She's in tip-top shape. Wouldn't take her more than fifteen minutes. She has her costume in her purse. Something easy to throw on, like a Hillary Clinton mask. She slips into the building with a bunch of young kids and their parents, unrecognized by Bullets who's sitting there on the sofa. Goes to the sixteenth floor and waits for Muriel to leave Alan's party, pushes her down the stairs, then skedaddles back downstairs and out the front door in her costume. Tosses it and Muriel's pocketbook in the trash on her way back to the multiplex, and is there in plenty of time to wait for your men to pick her up."

Very mulled it over for a moment, his head nodding, nodding.

I kept talking. "Obviously, the question that arises is why Myrna would suddenly want to kill her best friend of almost fifty years."

He waved me off. "Naw, that's no big. Based on my professional experience—I actually happen to do this for a living, you know—people kill their best friends all of the time. Almost as often as they kill their spouses. And Bullets did say Myrna was tough as nails. It plays. Totally plays. I'm liking it." He sipped his Bass, gazing out at the park. "Okay, what else is rattling around in your skull?"

"We know that Olivia hate, hate, hated Muriel. Do you think she's capable of murder?"

"Totally. The woman has no conscience at all. Neither does that prick of a husband of hers."

"He told us he hasn't, but do you think there's any chance that Gary really did figure out who engineered that embargo of Olivia's leather goods?"

"Possible, but unlikely. Muriel asked Myrna to contact one of her late husband's old business associates—someone who he'd met through Anastasia. Those guys know how to keep their mouths shut. And did you notice the way Sandy Panisch clammed up when we raised the subject?"

We sat sipping our beers in silence for a moment, listening to the rush hour traffic on Central Park West sixteen floors below.

"What about Bullets?" Very wondered aloud.

"There was always a doorman in the lobby when he was sitting there on the sofa waiting for Muriel. And even if he did manage to slip away, unnoticed, the question of why comes up. He was genuinely fond of Muriel, not to mention a loyal mob soldier."

"What if he got orders?"

"From whom? Who would want her dead after all of these years?"

"Fair enough," Very conceded. "Throw someone else at me."

"Raoul. He's the one who found her body. Maybe that's because he's also the one who pushed her."

"Why would he?"

"This building's his private yum-yum tree. Filled with young, pretty undocumented migrants like Rosalita who are expected to perform sexual favors for him. It's either that or a one-way ticket back to Guatemala. Maybe one of them resisted his advances and he raped her. Maybe Muriel heard about it and was planning to bring it up before the co-op board. They wouldn't take too kindly to having a rapist as their building superintendent. Raoul has a sweet setup here. He sure would hate to lose it, wouldn't you say?"

"I would, and that definitely plays. I like it." He sipped his beer in thoughtful silence for a moment before he said, "What do you know about the doormen?"

"Frank, the redhead, is a real talker. A fountain of gossip. I rarely come in contact with Harvey, the overnight man. Know nothing about him, aside from the fact that he's counting the days until his retirement. George is a bitter, unhappy guy. Plus he *kicked* Lulu the other day, which puts him on my all-time shit list. I asked Frank once what his deal was. He told me that George has a dark cloud hanging over him."

"What kind?"

"The compulsive gambling kind. Plus he drinks."

"The two usually go together."

"His wife divorced him. Kept their two-bedroom apartment in Inwood and has another man in her life now. George is living by himself in that illegal basement studio sublet on West Eighty-Second Raoul found for him."

"And what about the talker, Frank? Anything there?"

"One of Gary's corporate raids bankrupted the supermarket chain where Frank's sister had worked forever. She lost a union job with benefits and had to move in with Frank and his wife—and now she needs surgery and no longer has health insurance, meaning he'll have to pay for it. All of which would give Frank a rock- solid motive for wanting to shove *Gary* down those stairs, not Muriel. That doesn't mean he didn't have one. I just can't imagine what it would be."

Lulu sat up abruptly, jumped from the settee, and went scampering toward the front door, whooping.

A moment later I heard the key unlock the door and Merilee came in, her cheeks flushed from the brisk fall air. I wondered if I would ever get tired of seeing Merilee Nash walk in the door.

She bent down to hug Lulu. "Yes, sweetness, I missed you, too. I haven't seen you for hours and hours. Did you think I wasn't coming back? You are such a sweetie. Yes, you are."

"I hope you don't mind that there are two disreputable bums guzzling beer in your living room," I said to her.

"I certainly do mind, especially if you don't offer me one. Actually, make that a glass of Côtes du Rhône, please."

I fetched it for her while she took off the shearling-lined buckskin jacket she'd bought in Montana when she made the Redford movie and sat on the settee with Very, sweeping her gorgeous golden hair back from her forehead. She was wearing a cream-colored cashmere turtleneck, jeans, and cowboy boots. I love her in that outfit. Lulu climbed back onto the settee and burrowed next to her with her head in Merilee's lap, gleeful argle-bargle noises coming from her throat.

"And where have you boys been today?" she asked, scrunching Lulu's ears.

"Where *haven't* we been?" I handed her the glass of wine and sat back down. "We started out with a trip to a castle in scenic Great Neck, Long Island. From there it was back to midtown Manhattan to pay a call on the law offices of Panisch and Panisch. Then we spent some quality time right next door with Olivia Pennington Kates and her charming husband, Gary. And from there it was on to Alan Levin's, where we've just finished up. It may please you to know that while we were there, Gretchen showed up under the pretext of returning her keys, which she could have just left downstairs with Frank, and the two of them decided to talk. So the Lieutenant and I fled."

Merilee took a sip of her wine. "Do you think she might take him back?"

"Would you take him back?"

Her green eyes glittered at me. "I took you back, didn't I?"

"True, but you made me wait ten long, lonely years. Plus I also happen to be the first major new literary voice of the 1980s—not to mention attractive in a devil-may-care way that's reminiscent of a vintage Hollywood leading man. Don't just take my word for it. *Cosmo* said so in its July '83 issue."

"In answer to your question? Yes, I do think so."

Very looked at her in surprise. "Seriously?"

"Seriously. I think Gretchen loves Alan and realizes that he was Silly Putty in the hands of Olivia. It won't be easy for Gretchen to forgive him. He'll have to take full responsibility for his behavior. And a small part of her will still wonder if the real reason Alan's interested in her is because her father's a major Broadway producer. She's twenty-eight and a great catch. Alan's forty-two and a neurotic mess. She could do a lot better for herself, if you ask me. Not that you did."

"And you, my dearest dear? What did you and your agent cook up?"

"It's not a very interesting story. I'll tell you later." Merilee narrowed her gaze at me. "You look oddly peevish. What is it?"

"It's nothing."

"It's something."

"Okay, it's Olivia."

"What about her?"

"She was having nooners with Alan, who's built like a squeeze toy. And she got an instant case of the hots for our friend Very here. Even managed to let him have a good look at her nipples twice.'"

"Three times," Very corrected me.

"Her *nipples*?"

"She was wearing one of those loose-fitting scoop-necked sweaters with nothing underneath it. Made a special point of repeatedly bending over the coffee table so he'd get a good, unobstructed look. Me, all I got was the merest of side glimpses."

"Forgive me, darling, but is there a point to this?"

"I was here by myself working on my book for six whole weeks while you were in Budapest, and not once did she hit on me. She didn't even say hello to me in the elevator."

Merilee gave me a not-exactly warm look. "Are you suggesting you would have slept with her?"

"I most definitely am not. I'm saying that I would have appreciated the chance to turn her down."

"Ah, I see." She smiled knowingly. "That's your answer right there. You would have turned her down, and she knew that."

"How?"

"Because women know these things. She could tell that you wouldn't have groveled and slobbered at the chance to climb aboard the great Olivia Pennington Kates. Why would you? You're already involved with *me*, and I happen to be way, way out of her aging debutante league, in case you haven't noticed. I'm an international star of stage and screen. I'm tall, blonde, not bad looking . . ."

"Gorgeous, if I may be allowed to say so."

"You may."

I tugged at my ear. "Do you really think that's the reason?"

"I do."

"Well, then in that case, I feel much better. Thank you, Merilee."

"My pleasure." She arched an eyebrow at Very. "Lieutenant, you aren't actually interested in her, are you?"

"Not a chance," he said emphatically. "I'd never do anything to hurt Norma."

"You're a good man," Merilee said approvingly.

The house phone rang.

Merilee lifted Lulu's head from her lap, got up, and went to the kitchen to answer it. "Yes . . . ? Is that so . . . ? Yes, he's right here. I'll be sure to tell him." She returned to us and said, "Lieutenant, that was Frank. Trevor Ferraro just came sidling into the lobby, made his way up to the reception desk, and asked if his Aunt Muriel is home."

Very shook his head. "You've got to be kidding me."

"He told Trevor she's not home right now but suggested that he have a seat and wait for her. So Trevor's sitting there waiting for her. Frank thought you'd want to know."

CHAPTER SIX

Trevor was seated in the permanent indentation that had been left behind in the lobby sofa by Bullets's humongous rear end. Bullets and his humongous rear end weren't occupying the sofa anymore because Bullets didn't have a job anymore. Trevor's knees were jiggling. He was also shivering. Wasn't wearing much for a brisk November day that was turning into night—just a plain white T-shirt that was at least four sizes too large for him, sweatpants, and a pair of baby-blue terry cloth slip-ons with no socks. He was paying zero attention to the police crime scene vans that were parked out front, or to the pair of patrolmen who were stationed out on the sidewalk, moving people along. He seemed oblivious to them and to just about everything else. His hair was uncombed. His face was covered with lesions.

Lulu ambled over and nudged his knee with her large black nose to say hi.

Trevor was so spaced out it took him a moment to notice her. "Oh, wow, a *dog*." He held his small, wavering hand out to her. She sniffed at it, then let out a displeased snuffle and backed away from him. She didn't like what she'd smelled.

The building's front door opened and George Strull hurried in wearing a New York Jets warm-up jacket and jeans. Lulu immediately let out a low growl. She hadn't forgotten what he'd done to her.

George darted behind the reception desk and started toward the doormen's break room to change into his uniform. "Don't say it," he blustered at Frank. "I'm a few minutes late, I know."

Frank made an elaborate show of looking at his watch. "Try an hour."

"I had to run an errand. Cut me some slack, will ya?"

"Show up on time for your shift and I will," Frank said irritably before he phoned home to tell his wife that he'd be home late for dinner.

Very and I sat in the armchairs that flanked the sofa where Trevor was parked.

"Hi, Trevor," I said. "How's it going?"

He peered at me, squinting slightly. "I know you. You were here when the shithead doorman wouldn't let me in. Your dog, too. Were her ears that big then?"

"They haven't grown since the last time you saw her, if that's what you're wondering."

He picked at his face, gazing blankly at Very. "I don't know you."

"I'm Detective Lieutenant Romaine Very of the NYPD. I'm a homicide investigator."

Trevor sat there in dazed silence for a long moment. Really long moment. "Homicide. Is that like . . . murder?"

"That's exactly like murder."

"What are you doing here?"

"My job."

Trevor glanced out the front window, noticing the crime scene vans and patrolmen for the first time. "So, like, someone got killed?"

"Your Aunt Muriel, I'm sorry to inform you."

Trevor shook his head at him. "Say *what*?"

"Your Aunt Muriel is dead."

"You're lying!"

"No, it's true, Trevor," I said. "Someone pushed her down the service stairs on the sixteenth floor. Broke her neck."

167

He gaped at me in wide-eyed disbelief. "You mean she's . . . gone?"

I nodded. "Gone."

"Happened last evening at around eight o'clock," Very said, eyeing him carefully. "There were Halloween festivities going on in the building. Open house parties on every floor. Kids trick-or-treating."

"Right, right. It was Halloween . . ." Trevor drifted away for a second before he said, "And Aunt Muriel is really dead?"

"Really dead," Very told him.

He let out an anguished cry and began to sob, tears streaming from his eyes. He wiped them on the sleeve of his T-shirt.

Frank brought him a Kleenex box from the reception desk. Trevor helped himself to one and blew his runny nose.

George returned from the break room in his uniform. Once again I noticed how, unlike Frank, he seemed to shrivel inside of his.

Frank started hurriedly for the break room to change clothes. "Okay, I'm out of here."

"Would you mind sticking around for a few more minutes?" Very asked him. "There are some questions I'd like to ask you. Both of you. Harvey, too. One of my men is picking him up at his apartment in Kew Gardens. They should be here soon."

"But the wife's waiting dinner for me, Lieutenant," he protested, shooting another displeased look at George.

"I'll make it as quick as I can."

"Sure, Lieutenant," Frank sighed. "Whatever you need."

Trevor swiped at his eyes, sniffling. "She was . . . she was good to me."

I said, "If by that you mean she didn't have your butt thrown in juvenile detention for stealing her jewelry, then, yeah, she was good to you. But she did order the doormen to not let you in anymore when she wasn't around. I was here when Frank told you to leave. You weren't real happy about that."

"Sounds to me like maybe you and your aunt weren't getting along so good," Very said to him, keeping his voice gentle.

"She was mad at me, it's true. But I got this problem, man, and I need money and she wouldn't let me have any."

"Which made you angry," Very suggested, continuing to keep his voice gentle. "So angry that you pushed her down those stairs last night."

"Right . . ." Trevor sat there picking at his face. "Wait, *what?* I didn't have anything to do with that. I wasn't even here, I swear!"

"So where were you?" Very demanded roughly, abruptly switching gears on him. "And can anyone vouch for your whereabouts?"

"Well, yeah. I was in Bellevue."

"You've been in the hospital?"

That would explain Lulu's displeased grunt when she'd sniffed his hand. She had unhappy memories of time spent in the hospital not long ago. We both did.

"I passed out, like, when I was crossing Second Avenue sometime yesterday afternoon. A cab driver saved me. Threw me in the back seat of his cab, drove me to Bellevue, and told them if he hadn't slammed on his brakes he would have, like, run me over. Or at least that's what they told me. I was so out of it I didn't remember a thing. They hooked me up to an IV bag and shot me up with something that put me to sleep. When I woke up this morning, they threw me in the shower and gave me these clothes. Then I had to talk to a shrink. He wants me to enter a drug program. I'm supposed to see some guy, um, tomorrow?" Trevor reached into the pocket of his sweatpants and pulled out an appointment card. He handed it over. Very showed it to me. It was indeed a Bellevue Hospital appointment card with a Doctor Kahn at 11:00 a.m. tomorrow.

Very handed it back to him. "They didn't want to keep you there in the drug ward?"

"Couldn't. Don't have enough beds."

"So where will you go tonight? Do you have a place to crash?"

Trevor shrugged his narrow shoulders. "Been crashing with a bro who has a place in the East Village."

"Where in the East Village?

"Um, East Ninth Street."

Very handed Trevor his notepad and a pen. "Write down his name, address, and phone number for me."

Trevor gazed down at the notepad dumbly. "His name's Loki. I, like, don't know his phone number. His place is in the middle of the block. A yellow building."

"Please correct me if I'm wrong," Very said. "But it sounds to me like you and your bro, Loki, pass out wherever you end up when you're high on crystal meth—which, lately, has been in a yellow building on East Ninth."

"I guess," he said, shivering. His scrawny arms had goose bumps on them.

Very studied him curiously. "When's the last time you had a decent meal, kid?"

"Don't have much of an appetite for food."

Very stood up and waved an arm at one of the patrolmen out front.

The patrolman hurried inside right away. "Help you, Loo?" He was a powerfully built young black guy, eager to make a good impression. Romaine Very was someone who had a lot of pull.

"Would you do me a huge favor and run Trevor up to the house?"

"You got it, Loo."

"See if you can find him some warmer clothes and shoes from the locker." Very dug a five-dollar bill from the pocket of his jeans and handed it to him. "And get him a cheeseburger, will you?"

"I told you, I'm not hungry," Trevor protested.

"You're still going to eat something."

"What do I do with him after that, Loo?"

"Put him in a holding cell. He's so spaced he may know something valuable and not know that he knows it. I also want to confirm that he was at Bellevue when he says he was."

"What do I charge him with?"

Very thumbed his chin. "You have any ID on you, Trevor?"

Trevor's eyes had glazed over. "ID?"

"You know, like a driver's license?"

"I'm fifteen, man. Don't have one yet."

"Have you got a wallet?"

"Not really."

"Well, what *have* you got on you?"

"Um, that card for the shrink appointment and . . ." Trevor fished around in the pocket of his sweatpants and found some loose change. "I got . . . sixty-seven cents."

Very grinned at him. "Congratulations, you've hit the big time. You're no longer just another zombie tweaker."

Trevor looked at him in bewilderment. "What am I?"

"A vagrant." To the patrolman he said, "Book him."

"Can you give me a quick run-through of your Halloween security protocol?" Very asked Frank and George.

"No problem, Lieutenant," Frank said as he changed out of his uniform. "We do the same thing every Halloween."

We'd moved to the doormen's break room, which was located in a short corridor behind the reception desk, because Frank was so anxious to change out of his uniform and get home. There were two other doors in the corridor. One belonged to Raoul's apartment. The other led to the basement.

"What's this about Halloween?" asked George, who was standing in the doorway to the reception desk, keeping his eyes on the lobby.

"He's asking about our security setup." Frank hung his uniform on a clothing rack and got into his own clothes—a heavy wool buffalo plaid shirt, jeans, and scuffed work boots. I'd never seen him out of uniform before, I realized. He looked like a completely different person. If I'd bumped into him on the street, I would have figured him for a long-haul trucker.

The doormen's break room was by no means luxurious. Aside from the clothing rack, there was a three-drawer dresser where they stored their fresh white shirts and gloves, a mini fridge, microwave oven, small dinette with three chairs, and a beat-up recliner. There was also a small lavatory.

"Hey, look who the cat dragged in," George said as I heard slow, heavy footsteps approaching the reception desk.

Harvey Buchalter joined us in the break room, looking none too happy to be there. The short, stout, senior member of the trio was puffy eyed with sleep, his white hair was uncombed. He wore a blue peacoat and baggy khakis.

"Hey there, Harve," Frank said, smiling at him.

"Thanks for coming in, Harvey," Very said. "Appreciate it."

"Y'know, I'm supposed to be asleep right now, Lieutenant," he complained. "I'm not due to report for my shift until two in the morning. Some cop just came pounding on my door, woke me up, and told me to get dressed and come with him, pronto. When I'm done here, I'll have to schlep back home to Kew Gardens, catch the rest of my zees, and then schlep right back again. This isn't fair."

"I'm genuinely sorry to put you out, but I've got a lady in Sixteen-D who didn't wake up today. In fact, she's never going to wake up. I'm afraid that takes priority over your beauty sleep."

"Why don't you save yourself a trip and sack out here in the recliner, Harve?" Frank suggested. "There's an old blanket around somewhere. Just close the door and turn out the light. It'd be a lot easier."

"I may do that," Harvey groused as he became aware that Lulu was sniffing daintily at the cuffs of his pants. "What's your dog doing to my leg?"

"Just her way of saying hello. Do you live alone in Kew Gardens?"

"Why, you got a girl for me?"

"That's it, Harve, don't lose your sense of humor," kidded Frank, who seemed genuinely fond of the old fellow.

Lulu finished sniffing at Harvey's cuffs and stretched out under the dinette without making a sound. Evidently she hadn't picked up a scent that was of any interest—though she can be cagey sometimes.

"Did you know Muriel well?" Very asked Harvey.

He shook his head. "Don't think I saw her more than a handful of times in all of the years I been here. She wasn't a night owl or early riser. Last time I saw her was when I took George's shift while he was on vacation back in March."

"April," George said from the doorway.

"One evening," Harvey recalled, "she came rolling home at ten o'clock or so in that Rolls-Royce of hers. What a car. Must be worth a fortune."

"Ever meet her chauffeur?"

"Who, Bullets? Yeah, sure. He'd wait for her on the sofa like a big, ugly statue. Not move. Not say hello. Just wheeze. What a piece of work."

"Where'd you go on your vacation?" Very asked George.

"What do you care?" George answered coldly.

"Okay, that's not how this works, George." Very's jaw went to work on a fresh piece of bubble gum. "I ask questions, you answer them. Got it?"

George shrugged, his eyes never leaving the front door. "Vegas."

"Have a good time?"

"Got laid, lost all of my money. It was Vegas." The man positively oozed with charm. Though he did manage to summon something vaguely approximating a smile as he called out, "Evening, Mr. Whitesides."

"Evening, George," responded a resident who'd evidently arrived home.

Raoul appeared in the break room doorway now from his apartment, sized up the situation, and said, "George, why don't I watch the door for you? No sense you trying to do two things at once."

"Sure," George grunted, joining Frank and Very at the dinette with his arms crossed before him.

Lulu immediately let out a low growl and moved over by the doorway, watching George balefully. Harve settled wearily in the recliner. I remained standing. I'd been sitting all day.

Very turned to Frank and said, "So tell me about your security setup on Halloween night."

"Sure thing," Frank said, glancing at his watch. "For starters, all three of us were on duty to make sure that there'd be a man on the door at all times. Harve and I both pulled overtime."

"I ran the elevator to maintain a semblance of order," Harvey said. "You would not believe how out of control a bunch of rich ten-year-old brats can get when they're high on sugar. And we don't want nobody to get hurt. Besides, I'm too old to be a cruiser."

"A cruiser?"

"George and I alternated every half hour," Frank explained. "One of us would stay on the front door while the other cruised the corridors and stairwells for disturbances."

"What kind of disturbances?"

"Kids acting up," George said.

"And were they?"

He nodded. "Of course. They're kids. I caught the Bernstein brothers from 10D in the service stairs smoking pot. Twelve, thirteen years old, and already they're getting high. I dragged 'em home. Their father's some kind of rock concert promoter. He was so stoned himself he didn't even give a shit."

Frank said, "And I caught a couple of younger girls, maybe ten, smoking cigarettes on the fourth-floor stairs. One of them lives here. Her father's a federal judge. The other girl I didn't know. They behave like little angels in the corridors when Harve lets them out of the elevator—aside from all of the candy wrappers they toss on the carpet and expect us to pick up for them. But the real action is in the stairwell. Ask Raoul. He'll tell you how many cigarette butts he found."

"He also found Muriel," I said.

Frank's face dropped. "Yeah. Sad business. I'm going to miss her smile in the morning. Hell, I'm even going to miss Bullets. But it was a typical Halloween—aside from Muriel, that is." He glanced at his watch again. "Are we about done here, Lieutenant?"

"Almost. Is that pretty much your take on things, too?" Very asked George.

George said, "I guess. We want the kids to have a good time. That's not so easy for kids growing up in a high-rise building. I lived in one in the Bronx with my brothers before we moved into a house out on the Island. It wasn't much. Just an El Cheapo cracker box in Patchogue. But we loved it out there. Rode our bikes around the neighborhood, tossed a football around with our friends." A rare glint of pleasure brightened his glum face before it vanished so quickly it was as if it had never been there at all. "Kids need to run around without somebody always looking over their shoulder. It's not like when you grow up in a high-rise. Even a mink-lined one like this one."

"Did any of you see Muriel's nephew, Trevor?"

"I didn't," Frank said.

"Me neither," George said.

"How about you?" Very asked Harvey.

"Wouldn't know him. I've never met him. Besides, it was Halloween, remember? He could have been dressed up like Frankenstein's monster and snuck in with a bunch of other kids."

"Fair point, although I'm not sure Trevor's that swift between the ears." Very turned to Frank. "Did a lot of adults show up from somewhere else so that their kids could trick-or-treat here with their friends? Or maybe to attend one of the open house parties?"

"It was pretty hectic between five thirty and six," Frank acknowledged. "And then again at around eight when the open house parties were winding down. Everyone had to sign in and out at the desk. Quite a few adults had been invited to the parties. Some came in costume, some not."

"Like you, for instance," George said to Very pointedly. "I was on the door when you signed in. You weren't wearing a costume. Neither was that skinny little broad you brought with you."

"She's not a 'broad,'" Very said to him coldly. "She's one of the top editors in the publishing business. And she's not skinny either. She's slender."

George shrugged. "Whatever you say. Didn't mean any disrespect."

"Like hell you didn't. Frank, is that sign-in sheet still around?"

"You bet, Lieutenant. It's on a clipboard at the front desk."

"Mind if I borrow it for a day? I'll bring it back."

"Sure, no problem."

"A stab in the dark—do you happen to remember signing in a tall, older woman wearing a costume?"

Frank thought about it for a second before he shook his head. "Not offhand. But she would have signed in and out."

"I don't think she would have used her real name."

"May I ask who we're talking about?" Frank asked.

"Muriel's friend, Myrna Waldman."

"Oh, sure. Myrna came by to visit Muriel lots of times. If I'd seen her, I'd remember—unless she had on a costume, like you say. Do you think she was here last night?"

"Just considering all of the possibilities. You said things got hectic again at around eight?"

"Yeah. It was a Sunday evening. A school night. The parents wanted their kids home early. Harve didn't let any more trick-or-treaters on the elevator after eight o'clock. Posted a sign in the lobby by the elevator door that the festivities were over. Then he took over the front desk while me, George, and Raoul went from floor to floor to shut down the open house parties as tactfully as we could. If the adults were still enjoying themselves, that was fine. We just asked them to please close their doors. But most of them were already winding down. The residents here are busy professional people. Not necessarily close friends with their neighbors. Honestly? We thought we had everything buttoned up good and tight. Right up until Raoul made his last pass of the service stairs for any stragglers—and reached the fifteenth-floor landing."

"It was . . . horrible, Lieutenant," Raoul recalled, seated at the big, gray steel desk in the living room of his apartment. "Her eyeballs, they were staring right at me. I thought I was going to throw up, I swear."

"That's nothing to be ashamed of," Very assured him. "I know cops with ten years on the job who still hurl at the sight of blood. It's a shock to your system."

"That it is, sir. That it is."

Raoul's apartment, a low-ceiling one-bedroom, wasn't a whole lot more luxurious than the doormen's break room next door. His steel desk, which was cluttered with multiple stacks of invoices, two Rolodexes, and two phones, was so dented that it looked as if he'd found it abandoned on a sidewalk somewhere and paid a couple of neighborhood teenagers to help him lug it home. Actually, the entire living room, what little there was of it, seemed to be furnished with found objects or cast-offs left behind by former residents. The walnut veneer on his dining table was peeling off. Not one of his four dining chairs matched another. His avocado-colored vinyl sofa had seen better days, and even those days hadn't been very good days.

"Do me a favor and think carefully, will you?" Very said to him. "When you were on, say, the tenth or twelfth floor of the service stairs, making your last pass for stragglers, do you remember hearing anything?"

Raoul furrowed his brow. "Like what?"

"A scuffle, a thud, maybe the footsteps of someone running away. This would have been *before* you were aware of what had happened up on fifteen and wouldn't necessarily have thought much of it at the time. Figured it was merely kids fooling around. Did you hear anything like that?"

The slim building super sat there in his neatly pressed khaki uniform and furrowed his brow some more. "No, I'm afraid not. Such a terrible thing. Eleven years I've been here, and the security has always been first-rate. No muggings, no break-ins. This is so upsetting."

I sat at the dining table next to Very and studied Raoul, who I'd learned was three, three, three men in one. He was polite to the point of unctuous around the building's co-op owners. He was crafty to the point of slippery around tradesmen. And he was a consummate sleaze when it came to collecting gossip and sexual favors from maids and housekeepers. The man was an operator.

Was he also a murderer?

Lulu didn't like him, I can tell you that much. She stayed perched on her haunches by the door, watching him guardedly.

"How much did you know about Muriel?" Very asked him.

Raoul shook his head at him. "Know about her?"

"I gather she was a woman of some means. Chauffeur-driven antique Rolls-Royce and all."

Raoul paused for a moment, running a hand over his thinning hair before he said, "I know very little. Muriel never talked about herself. I assumed she was a wealthy widow. She didn't pay any of her bills herself. Her lawyer, a Mr. Panisch, took care of the monthly maintenance check on her apartment, her utilities, and so on. I don't believe I ever saw her write a check, and she didn't have any credit cards."

"How do you know that?"

"I once asked her for a credit card number so that I could place an order with a plumbing supply company for a new bathroom faucet that she wanted. She told me she didn't believe in credit cards, so I used my own card and she paid me back—in cash. She paid the plumber who installed it in cash, too. Crisp, new twenty-dollar bills."

"And how many of those crisp, new twenty-dollar bills did the plumber kick back to you?" Very asked, not bothering to be tactful.

Raoul frowned. "I do not know what you mean."

"Sure, you do. Every super I've ever met has kickback deals with plumbers, electricians, and other tradesmen so they'll get the first call from you when someone needs work done. Price of doing business for them."

He shrugged his shoulders. "If they wish to tip me, as a small courtesy, who am I not to accept it?"

"You also found George the doorman an illegal basement sublet on West Eighty-Second through a friend who's a fellow super. Did you get a small courtesy out of that, too?"

Raoul's mouth tightened. "Does the NYPD provide you with a pension plan, Lieutenant?"

"Yes, it does," Very answered. "Why?"

"I have no such pension plan myself. I have no retirement portfolio, either. Not like the wealthy people who live here. So whatever little extras I collect for myself, I put away in a savings account. A man has to take care of himself, does he not?"

"Tell me, did Panisch pay Muriel's housekeeper, Rosalita, by check, or did Muriel take care of her on her own?"

"Muriel paid Rosalita herself. Always with crisp, new twenty-dollar bills. Paid her most generously, I might add."

"And you got a piece of that, too?"

"A half dozen of the girls live at my sister's house rent-free," he responded, raising his chin slightly. "And they are here in the US without green cards. It's to be expected that I get a modest percentage of their income."

"I understand that's not all you get."

"Sorry? I do not understand."

"I'm told they're also expected to grant you sexual favors. If they don't, there's a threat hanging over them that you'll send them back to Guatemala."

Raoul's face colored angrily. "Who told you such filthy nonsense?"

"It's common knowledge around the building, Raoul," I said. "It's also common knowledge that they supply you with gossip. That's how Gretchen found out about Alan and Olivia. One of the housekeepers who works for Olivia told you, and then it got passed along to Gretchen by way of Alan's housekeeper. You've got yourself a first-class gossip mill here, not to mention your very own little harem. I understand that you're especially partial to teenagers like Rosalita."

He glared at me furiously. "You make me sound like an animal! Not once have I laid a hand on a woman who wasn't receptive to my advances. And I have never touched an underage girl."

"Seventeen is the legal age in New York. Rosalita can't be a day over that. And you're, what, forty-two?"

"I'm forty-four. What of it?"

"You're old enough to be her father. I find that kind of unsettling. How about you, Lieutenant?"

"Pervy is more like it."

Raoul sat there in furious silence for a moment. "The three of us here, we are all men, and I can speak plainly, can't I? We have needs, do we not?"

"I have a girlfriend who sees to mine," said Very.

"And I have a wife. Well, ex-wife." Lulu stirred, making small, unhappy noises. "It's complicated."

"I, myself, do not have a steady companion. This apartment is not ideal for sharing with another person. But I live here rent-free, which allows me to put money in my savings account every month. Soon I hope to have a proper home of my own. A wife and children. But this . . ." He looked around at his dingy little apartment. "This is a job for a single man."

"Your gossip mill stirs up plenty of trouble," Very said. "But how does that benefit your savings account?"

"Because it pays to be aware of what's going on. If a couple is talking about splitting up and putting their apartment on the market, I'm acquainted with a realtor who will pay me five hundred dollars to get first shot at the listing. If a gentleman is cheating on his wife, I can tactfully point out that he ought to be more discreet, because

I'm hearing whispers. Possibly he'll thank me by giving me free courtside seats to a Knicks game, which I can then scalp for a considerable sum."

"Is it just me or does that sound like blackmail?" I said to Very.

"Most definitely," he agreed.

Raoul shook his head. "I don't see it that way."

"Of course you don't," Very said.

"I'm merely letting the gentleman know what I'm hearing."

"Of course you are. They must be able to figure out that you're hearing about it from their housekeepers."

"Possibly. But they would never take it out on one of my girls. If they did, they would have to answer to me."

I tugged at my ear. "So you not only take sexual advantage of them, but you're their protector, too. The kindly uncle type. Quite some setup you've got here, Raoul. I'm impressed. Very."

The Lieutenant glanced over at me. "Yeah, what is it, dude?"

"I'm very impressed."

"Yo, that goes double for me."

Raoul said, "I don't wish to presume, Lieutenant, but may I suggest you have a chat with some of the other supers on Central Park West? Every single one of them has side deals by the dozen. I am like an amateur in comparison."

"Sure, you are." Very climbed to his feet. "Thank you for your time."

"It was no trouble at all," Raoul said with a distinct lack of warmth. "Allow me to show you out."

"Not necessary," Very said, starting for the door.

Lulu was plenty anxious to leave. She didn't like the vibes in there. She wasn't the only one.

The doormen's break room door was shut. Possibly Harvey was grabbing some zees in that recliner. George was on the front desk. He nodded to us in sour silence as we strolled past him into the lobby.

"Stay with me," Very said, heading out the door into the chill of the evening. Lulu and I stayed with him. He paused under the awning in thoughtful silence, his head nodding, nodding. "There's something distasteful about that guy."

"That would be because he's a total sleazebag."

"A total sleazebag who could have pushed Muriel down those stairs himself for the contents of her alligator pocketbook—he has no pension plan, you know—then come running to your apartment to tell me that he'd just found her." Very stood there, his wheels turning. "I like him for it, gotta say. I like him a lot."

"What did he do with her pocketbook?"

"Tossed it somewhere. Who knows? I could get a warrant to search that shithole apartment of his, but it won't be there. Neither will the cash. He's no dope. He's one clever dude. But I don't have a shred of evidence that he did it. Nothing on him that, strictly speaking, qualifies as criminal behavior. Just suspicions. And the sleaze factor."

"The man's a building super, Lieutenant. Sleaze is an essential part of the job description. I've never met one yet whom you'd mistake for Mister Rogers. What's your next move?"

"I'm heading back to the house now to find out if I can get anything coherent out of Trevor."

"Want me along?" I heard a low cough at my feet. "Us along?"

"Not necessary. Spend some quality time with Merilee."

"And what about tomorrow?"

"I'll be working the case and you'll be working on your novel. What's that ritual of yours? Up at dawn? At your typewriter by six thirty with a cup of hot espresso and the Ramones blasting away?"

"That about covers it."

"Thanks for your help today, dude. Appreciate it."

"And thank you for your ace map-reading skills."

"Are you ever going to stop chumping me about that?"

"Don't know. I'll have to think about it. So we're done?"

"We're done."

"You sound awfully sure about this."

"That's because I'm positive I'll be wrapping this one up in no time." He tapped his forehead. "I've got a feeling."

"So have I."

"Which is . . . ?"

"That you'll be needing me again."

"If I do," Romaine Very said, "I know where to find you."

"So tell me already, will you?"

"Tell you what, darling?"

"Your not very interesting story about who's taking over as director of *The Sun Also Rises*."

"Oh, that."

We were having dinner at Tony's because when I'd asked her what she was in the mood for, she'd said "anything but goulash." So Tony's it was. My regular waiter, Bruno, was so delighted to see Merilee walk in the door with Lulu and me that he brought us a bottle of their very best Chianti Classico—on the house—and made a huge fuss about what an honor it was to serve her. He never told me it was an honor to serve me. Or brought me a bought of their best Chianti Classico on the house. But, hey, being a movie star does have its advantages. He even brought us a tasty hot antipasto platter that wasn't on the menu.

Merilee and I both ordered veal piccata. Lulu stayed with her usual fried calamari. She's a hound of steady habits, including circling under the table three times before she curled up on my feet.

"Mike Nichols has turned it down," Merilee said after we'd clinked glasses. "So has Sydney Pollack."

"Well, that certainly didn't take long."

"Convincing someone to say yes takes forever. Saying no takes five minutes. The studio has a list of four directors. If none of them says yes, then they're prepared to eat the cost of the location shooting we've done in Budapest and scrap the whole project. Sounds crazy, I know, but Budapest's actually the least of it in terms of money and time. We haven't filmed any of the interiors in London yet. The sets haven't even been built. And we haven't shot the sequences in Pamplona, which will be the most elaborate and expensive. Meanwhile, Mel is on a tight schedule. His next *Lethal Weapon* goes into production at the beginning of April." She took a sip of her wine, sighing morosely. "I'm beginning to fear that *The Sun Also Rises* will turn into one of those unfinished oddities like Orson Welles was doodling around with in the twilight of his career, destined to be unearthed and pored over by so-called film scholars when I'm old and gray."

"But not enormously fat."

"I certainly hope not, although that *is* a viable option. Shelley Winters made a whole second career for herself playing fat, angry cows."

"Merilee, I don't want you jetting away again, but I'd also hate to see all of that work you've done go to waste. That's just plain crazy." I sampled a little confection of sausage and cheese baked inside a flaky pastry that was so delicious I wondered why Bruno had been hiding it from me all these months. *Because you're not an Oscar-winning movie star, butthead, that's why.* "Tell me, would you be willing to work with your original director?"

"I absolutely would. He and I had some creative differences, but we ironed them out."

"Could you convince the studio suits to reverse course and rehire him?"

"Funny you should mention that. As it happens, that's exactly what Geoff, my agent, and I were discussing. I'm going to throw my weight behind giving him a second chance. So is Mel, who it turns out is a very loyal person. We're also represented by the same agency. If we stick together, with the agency's clout behind us, it wouldn't be a wise move for them to piss us off. Hollywood's a small town. Word gets around fast."

Bruno brought us our veal piccata with roasted potatoes and sautéed spinach.

I dove right into my veal, savoring every tender, delicious morsel. "But would he swallow his pride and agree to come back?"

Merilee responded with a cascade of laughter.

I looked down at Lulu. Lulu was looking up at me. "Did I say something funny?"

"Sometimes I forget how different our two businesses are," she answered as she ate. "Authors have genuine pride and self-respect. Not one person in the movie business does. We pretend that we do, but that's just a put-on. We've all been lied to, shat upon, cheated out of money, stabbed in the back, stabbed in the front . . . Whatever pride we may have possessed is long gone. Trust me, he'd crawl across broken glass on his hands and knees to get a chance to finish directing this movie." She sipped her wine, her green eyes studying me. "You seem terribly serious, darling. Is it because of Muriel?"

I sipped my wine, mulling it over. "I suppose. I was fond of her, and it turns out she was Albert Anastasia's slice on the side who was living on gobs of Murder, Inc., blood money that he'd stashed away for her before he got plugged in the barbershop of the Park Sheraton. That sweet old lady and her Silver Cloud have been Gambino-family funded for the past thirty-six years. Do you know what she was doing when she met her beloved Albert? She was a hatcheck girl at the Copa. And her elegant friend Myrna, the one who now lives in a castle in Great Neck, was a cigarette girl."

Merilee cut into her veal, chewing on it thoughtfully. "Times were hard. They were pretty girls with no social advantages and probably not much education who did whatever they had to do to get by. I think it's unfair to judge them by today's standards. Someone like Olivia Pennington Kates, on the other hand, is an entirely different story."

"Olivia? What about her?"

"She was blessed with every social, educational, and financial advantage a woman could possibly dream of, and yet she has absolutely no sense of personal morality and is married to a Harvard Business School graduate who gets rich by destroying other peoples' lives. He may not gun them down in hotel barbershops, but ask yourself this—how many people have committed suicide or ended up addicted to drugs because of what Gary Kates did to them?"

I smiled at her. "I knew there was a reason I liked you."

Bruno stopped by to ask us if we were ready for another bottle of wine.

"Not for me, thanks," I said. "Tomorrow's a workday."

He nodded graciously and moved along.

"So it's back to your Olympia at dawn?" Merilee asked me.

"That's the general idea."

"And you're sure I don't distract you?"

"Positive."

She reached across the table and put her hand over mind. "Good, because I'm so delighted that you're living there again."

"As am I."

After we'd nibbled on chocolate biscotti with our espressos, we strolled home, me puffing on a Chesterfield while Lulu ambled happily ahead of us. George was on the front door, looking like his usual incredible shrinking self in his blue uniform and bellman's cap. The crime scene technicians' vans were gone. The cops in their blue-and-whites were gone. All was quiet.

"Good evening, George," Merilee said to him cheerily.

"Seems as if life's back to normal again," I observed.

"Not a moment too soon for me," he grumbled. "I didn't like having all of those cops here. Total strangers were coming in off the street to ask me what was going on, as if it's any of their damned business."

"New Yorkers are a congenitally nosy lot," I said.

"Nice to have you back, Miss Nash."

"Why, thank you, George."

As soon as the elevator closed Merilee grabbed me and kissed me. She does that. Just decides to get amorous without warning—not that I've ever had reason to complain, mind you. By the time we'd reached the sixteenth floor and made it inside the apartment, her turtleneck sweater was off, my cheviot wool trousers were down around my knees, and we were making a lip-locked, three-legged stumble for the bedroom, where we tore the rest of our clothes off and had a most enjoyable time before we collapsed in each other's arms shortly before midnight.

I felt as if I'd just fallen asleep when the phone rang. The nightstand clock said it was barely three o'clock. Merilee was out so cold she didn't even hear it. I fumbled for it, not quite awake. Heard a faint, distant voice. Realized I was holding the wrong end of the phone to my ear. Turned it around and heard a loud, clear voice say, "Are you there, dude?"

"Lieutenant . . . ?" I croaked. "It's the middle of the night. What's . . . going on?"

"What's going on is that I've been out scouring every skeegie bar on the Upper West Side for his bookie. Figured he's the type who wouldn't stray far from his home base, you know? And I was right, too. I finally—"

"Wait, wait. You're talking *really* fast and I'm a little lost. Actually, totally lost. Who are we talking about?"

"George, your doorman. The one who's a compulsive gambler and lives in an illegal basement sublet on West Eighty-Second. You with me now?"

I rubbed my eyes, yawning. "Uh, sure. Sort of."

"I finally found his bookie at the Dublin House on Amsterdam at one thirty. His name's Choo-Choo."

"That's his real name?"

"No, it's what he calls himself. His real name's Johnny Sicuranza."

"I prefer Choo-Choo."

"I'll be sure to tell him. When I showed him my shield, he got a panicked look on his face. I told him to chill. Just wanted to ask him some questions."

"And . . . ?"

Merilee stirred next me, yawning. "Who's that on the phone?"

"It's Very."

"Very what?"

"Lieutenant Very."

"What does he want at three in the morning?"

"He hasn't told me yet."

"Well, tell him I said hi. Also that I'm glad he'd never cheat on Norma."

Then she turned over and went back to sleep.

"Merilee says hi. So you found George's bookie, Choo-Choo, and . . . ?"

"And he told me that this afternoon at about five thirty, George paid off two of the four grand he was into him for—in crisp, new hundred-dollar bills."

I was much more awake now, recalling how irritated Frank had been when George showed up late for his five o'clock shift. "Where do you suppose he got those crisp, new hundred-dollar bills?"

"The same place you're supposing he got them—from Muriel Cantrell's pocketbook, which Raoul told us was gone when he found her on the stairs. I remembered that George clocks out at two a.m., and what with his apartment being a five-minute drive from the Dublin House, I headed on over there and . . ." Very broke off, breathing in and out.

"You headed on over there and . . . ?"

"I found him lying dead outside the door to his basement apartment. Somebody gutted him with a knife."

I felt my stomach muscles tighten involuntarily. "Where are you now, Lieutenant?"

"Still here. I called in the cavalry. The street's been cordoned off, medical examiner's on his way. And then I called you. Would you like to know why?"

"Do tell."

"Because George still has his wallet in his back pocket with forty-seven dollars in it. This was no random two a.m. mugging. This has Muriel written all over it. Listen, what would you say to—?"

"We'll be there in ten minutes." I hung up the phone and nudged Lulu. "Up and at 'em, girl. We're needed." She yawned hugely and climbed down from the bed while I went fumbling around in the darkness for a Viyella shirt, my torn jeans, and Werber flight jacket.

Merilee flicked on her nightstand lamp. "What is it, darling? Where are you going?"

"Somebody just stabbed George the doorman to death outside of his apartment."

A pained look creased her lovely face. "We just spoke to him in the lobby."

"I know."

"And now he's dead?"

"Couldn't be deader."

"What happened? Was he mugged?"

"Lieutenant Very doesn't think so."

"What do *you* think?"

"I think I'm not going to get very much writing done in the morning."

CHAPTER SEVEN

George's street was the usual mix of Yushied-up five-story brownstones and outright-slummy five-story brownstones that were to be found in the West Eighties between Columbus and Amsterdam Avenues. Some of the buildings had been spruced up and rent-jacked for the Young Urban Shitheads who'd been swarming all over the city like cockroaches for the past few years. Others, like my own up on West Ninety-Third, remained cheap, run-down dumps crammed with struggling actors, writers, musicians, and the other delightfully disreputable dreamers who make New York City the only city in America that's worth living in.

The sidewalks on West Eighty-Second were sprinkled with spindly ginkgo trees. Parked cars, none of them shiny or new, lined the curb on one side of the street, bumper to bumper. George's building, which was in the middle of the block, had escaped Yushification so far. In fact, it made my own place look upscale. His basement apartment, which had bars over its windows, was the sort that was accessed underneath the stoop.

Three blue-and-whites, an ME's van, and Very's unmarked, beat-up Crown Vic were double-parked out front, all of them with their lights on. The sidewalk had been cordoned off, and beefy patrolmen were shooing people along, not that there were many people strolling by at three in the morning. But the neighbors across the street were peering out their windows or standing on their stoops, the better to watch the show. The ME was in the process of examining George's body by the light of the open apartment door as well as a high-beamed flashlight his assistant was holding on the dead doorman, who'd slid down the wall and settled in the doorway, slumped over to one side. He was wearing the green Jets warm-up jacket and blue jeans he'd had on when he arrived for his evening shift. The lower half of his face was reddened and bruised, as if someone with a big hand had held it tightly over his mouth so that he couldn't cry out. His jacket was soaked with blood.

One of the cops gruffly ordered me to move along. When I told him that Lieutenant Very had summoned me there, he peered dubiously at me, then even more dubiously down at Lulu, before he allowed as how I'd find the Lieutenant inside the apartment. We went inside, being careful not to interfere with the ME. Found Very poking around in there, his head nodding to its own speed metal beat. The illegal sublet that Raoul had found for George had the cozy ambiance of a prison cell, thanks to those bars on the windows, which enjoyed a luxurious view of the building's trash cans. There was a mattress on the floor with a blanket and two pillows on it. No sheets or pillowcases. There was a television. There was a closet where a spare doorman's uniform and ski parka were hanging. A pair of suitcases lay open on the floor in there with the remainder of his clothing in them. There was a Pullman kitchen that had a sink full of dirty dishes. There was a small bathroom.

Lulu immediately got busy sniffing and snuffling her way around.

"Sorry to drag you out of bed, dude," Very said quietly.

"Not a problem. Happy to help. Well, not happy, but I want to do what I can. I'm thinking this has something to do with Muriel's murder. Is that what you're thinking?"

"Oh, yeah, it's the same case," he said. "I don't have a doubt in my mind."

After Lulu found nothing of interest except for a pair of dirty socks on the bathroom floor, she joined us, highly dissatisfied.

I looked out the barred windows at the neighbors across Eighty-Second Street, who were taking in this real-life crime drama from their windows and stoops. "Did anyone see or hear anything?"

"We're still canvassing, but yeah. The young woman who lives in the fourth-floor front apartment in the building directly across the street is an insomniac. She told a patrolman that while she was lying in bed trying to fall asleep she heard a car pull up outside at right around two o'clock and idle there for several minutes. Then she heard a car door open, and footsteps, and then a few minutes later the driver got back in and drove off."

"Did she hear voices, a scuffle . . . ?"

"She said no."

"How about the car? Could she tell him anything about what type it was?"

"She said it sounded like an American-made V-8, probably a Chevy. And that it sounded throaty, like it was going to need a new muffler soon."

"What is she, an auto mechanic?"

"No, an assistant editor at *Vogue*."

"That would certainly make me an insomniac."

"But her father is. A mechanic, that is."

"What was it Bullets told us he drove to and from Rego Park when he came to fetch Muriel's Silver Cloud from that garage on Columbus?"

"A Buick LeSabre," Very replied. "Red."

"Hmm . . . Not a Chevy, but it's made by GM and it's got a monster under the hood. Are you thinking what I'm thinking?"

"I seriously doubt it. Why, what are you . . . ?"

"Bullets found out."

Very frowned at me. "Found out what, dude?"

"That when the Halloween open houses were winding down, and George was circulating in the hallways, he ran into Muriel heading back to her apartment and tried to hit her up for a loan. Everyone knew she carried a lot of cash in that alligator pocketbook of hers. When she told George no, since she no doubt knew he was a compulsive gambler and would never pay her back, he made a grab for it. George was a desperate man. He *needed* that money to pay off Choo-Choo. When Muriel put up a struggle, which I have no doubt she would have, he pulled her into the stairwell, grabbed the pocketbook, and shoved her down the stairs."

"Okay, you're right," Very admitted with great reluctance. "I am thinking what you're thinking."

"That would also explain why he kicked Lulu hard enough to make her yelp. She would have picked up Muriel's scent on him and made a big fuss. I wonder if he made up that story about getting bit by a rabid dog when he was a kid or if that was total bullshit. He didn't strike me as the type to dream up something that elaborate right on the spot. Did he strike you as someone who'd dream up something that elaborate right on the—?"

"Dude, you're babbling."

"Forgive me. I'm not often summoned from my nice, warm king-sized bed in the middle of the night to a grisly murder scene. Any sign of Muriel's pocketbook?"

"I've got two men searching every trash can between here and your building. Nothing yet." Very glanced around George's bare basement studio, grimacing. "I don't know about you, but this place gives me the creeps. Let's go find a twenty-four-hour diner and get a cup of coffee."

"I have a much better idea."

I had to rap sharply on the glass front door to Merilee's building with my keys to rouse old Harvey, who was fast asleep on the lobby sofa. He got up slooowly, blinking and yawning, unlocked the door, and let us in.

As sleepy as he was, he could still tell from the looks on our faces that something was up. "What's going on, guys?"

"George Strull is dead," Very said to him.

Harvey gaped at him. "You kidding me?"

"Afraid not."

"Jeez . . ." Harvey slumped back down on the sofa, stunned. "What happened? Some gang of punks mug him on his way home?"

"Not exactly. He was knifed in the gut right outside the door of his apartment, and whoever did it wasn't interested in the forty-seven dollars he had in his wallet."

"Jeez . . ." Harvey ran a hand through his uncombed white hair, shaking his head. "Poor George."

"How did he seem to you when he left here at the end of his shift?"

Harvey didn't respond. Just sat there, breathing heavily in and out. He was taking the news hard.

"Are you okay, Harve?" I asked him gently.

After a long moment he said, "Sure, fine. I just . . . you work with a guy all of these years . . . "

"It's a jolt," I acknowledged.

"That's it exactly. A jolt."

Very hit rewind and tried again. "How did he seem to you when he left here at the end of his shift?"

"Who, George?" Harvey let out a yawn, treating us to the not-fresh scent of his old-man breath. "His usual sorry self. He wasn't a happy guy."

"Was he acting nervous or upset?"

"Not so's I noticed. Why, did he have a reason to be?"

Very glanced at his watch. "What time will Frank show up for his shift?"

"He goes on duty at eight o'clock. Usually gets here by seven thirty—except today's his day off. His backup, Steve, will be coming in."

"Any idea where Frank lives?"

"Woodside. Why?"

"The department likes us to deliver this kind of news in person if we can. It's pretty cold hearing it over the phone."

"There's a sheet in the break room that has all of our contact info. Want me to get it for you?"

"That would be great. Thanks."

Harvey got up off the sofa with a groan and moved slowly across the lobby, his feet shuffling slightly. Went behind the reception desk. Opened the door that led to the break room. Returned a moment later with a slip of paper that had Frank's address on it.

"Appreciate it," said Very, pocketing it.

"Lieutenant, why would someone want to do that to George?" Harvey wondered. "Did he owe the wrong people too much money or something?"

"That's what we're trying to figure out."

"Sorry we woke you," I said. "You can go back to sleep now."

"Who are you kidding? I won't sleep a wink."

We rode the elevator up to the sixteenth floor, and I let us into the apartment as quietly as I could. Lulu joined us in the kitchen for an anchovy while I put the espresso on. Then she headed for the master bedroom to climb back into bed with Merilee. I didn't blame her. That would have been my first, second, and third choice, too. I closed the bedroom door softly behind her. When the espresso was ready, I poured us two cups, and Very and I made our way down the long hallway to my office. I closed both the living room pocket door and the office door behind us. Even so, we kept our voices low as we took grateful sips of the strong espresso, Very seated in Lulu's leather chair, me at my desk.

"They had a bit of a history, those two," I said. "George and Bullets, I mean."

"Is that right? What kind?"

"Frank told me that George got curious some time back and asked Bullets what Muriel's story was. Bullets politely asked him to step outside and proceeded to drive a giant fist into George's side. Cracked three ribs—plus Frank said George was pissing blood for a week. That took care of his curiosity."

"Hmm." Very sipped his espresso. "Maybe it did, maybe it didn't."

"Let's say Bullets is our man . . ."

Very nodded. "Let's. He's definitely our prime suspect, considering he was Muriel's chauffeur for twelve years and was intensely loyal to her. He's also an old-time enforcer who has plenty of notches on his belt. And that V-8 engine our *Vogue* editor heard idling outside of George's apartment could have belonged to his Buick LeSabre."

"All true," I acknowledged. "But how did Bullets figure out that it was George who shoved Muriel down those stairs?"

"Same way I did—from George's bookie, Choo-Choo. Bullets still has contacts all over town. He's the one who located the jewelry that Trevor stole from Muriel, don't forget. So maybe he made some phone calls. So maybe Choo-Choo mentioned to a mutual friend that George paid him two-grand today in crisp, new hundred-dollar bills. The exact same kind of bills that Muriel carried in her pocketbook. To Bullets that would mean one thing and one thing only—that it was George who killed her.

How the hell else would George suddenly score two grand? Bullets had gone home to Rego Park by then, I'm assuming. So he grabbed a knife from the kitchen, drove his LeSabre back to the Upper West Side, and waited there on West Eighty-Second for George to get home from his shift. He was plenty well acquainted with the man's schedule. Plus that all fits with what the ME told me at the murder scene."

"Which was . . . ?"

"That George's killer was big and strong, and that he stuck him with a long, sharp kitchen knife, most likely a carving knife—although he wasn't positive about that last part. Didn't want to remove it until he got George on the examining table."

"The killer left the knife in him?"

Very nodded. "Drove it deep into George's gut, gave it a twist for good measure, and left it there. And he'd clamped a big hand over George's mouth to keep him from letting out a scream. The whole lower half of George's face was red. His mouth was bruised."

"I noticed."

"He also wore gloves. Left no prints behind on the handle of the knife."

"Sounds as if we can eliminate her nephew, Trevor, the runt."

"He's in a holding cell at the two-four for the night, remember?"

"But his friend Loki isn't. Maybe he's a big, strong guy."

"Maybe." Very gazed out the window at the predawn darkness of Central Park. "But he's also a brain-dead tweaker same as Trevor. And, just for the sake of discussion, let's say Trevor called Loki from the precinct house and told him to bump off George. How would Trevor have found out about George? How would he know where George lived? And is he together enough between the ears that it would even occur to him to avenge his aunt's murder? Nope, don't buy it."

"I don't either. I'm just considering all of the possibilities."

"Which is smart." Very flashed a grin at me. "I'm finally rubbing off on you."

"Any chance that Choo-Choo could be behind it?"

"Wouldn't think so. George had just handed over a healthy chunk of money. Why do away with him now?"

"Okay, then let's come at this from a different direction," I said, sipping my espresso. "What if it was someone else who killed Muriel—as in *not* George—and George knew about it and was holding him up for money?"

"That plays," Very conceded. "You have anyone specific in mind?"

"Raoul. He's the one who found Muriel's body on the fifteenth-floor landing, after all. Maybe the reason he found it is because he's the one who shoved her down those stairs. Maybe George witnessed it when he was making the rounds. You did say the ME thinks someone big and strong knifed George, and I'll admit that Raoul's not exactly Evander Holyfield. But he's wiry, had the element of surprise on his side, and if he was wearing a pair of heavy work gloves, they would have reddened the bottom of George's face that way."

Very considered this carefully, thumbing his chin. "I don't like Raoul for killing the old lady. He has himself too sweet a setup here. This whole building's his oyster. Why would he risk messing with that?"

"Maybe Muriel found out something about him that could have gotten him fired. Or possibly even worse."

"Such as . . . ?"

"Such as that maybe he raped one of those young Guatemalan housekeepers. Or maybe one of them is under legal age, which would mean he committed statutory rape. That's a felony."

"I'm aware of this, dude. I'm a police officer, remember?"

"Muriel was no shrinking violet. If she thought Raoul did wrong by any of those girls, she would have told him straightaway that she was taking it to the co-op board.

Possibly the police, too. So Raoul killed her to shut her up. Stole her nice, fat pocketbook for good measure. The man is plenty greedy. He has no pension, you know."

"But does he have a car?"

"Could have borrowed one from one of his pals. It's also possible that the Chevy V-8 our *Vogue* editor heard idling outside of George's at two a.m. had nothing whatsoever to do with George. Maybe a jealous boyfriend was buzzing his girlfriend to find out if she was really sick in bed like she told him she was."

"I would never, ever do that to Norma. I trust her and she trusts me."

"Is it my imagination or did we just segue into another conversation about you and your love life?"

Very chose to ignore that remark. Either that or he wasn't listening to me anymore. He seemed lost in thought. After a long moment, he drained the last drops of his espresso and said, "Okay, you talked me into it. We need to have another sit-down with Raoul. Is there anyone else in play? Tell me about Frank."

"He's a third-generation Irish American doorman from Queens. Outgoing, cheerful. A bit of a gossip, but a good guy. Also a big guy with big hands and big money troubles."

"I thought those doormen have a strong union. Make good bucks."

"They do. He does. But don't forget he also has an unmarried sister who just lost her own unionized supermarket job of thirty-two years thanks to Gary Kates's corporate pillaging. And if that had been Gary lying dead on the fifteenth-floor landing instead of Muriel, I'd point my finger right at Frank because he has to foot the bill for his sister's operation. He's also got a son who's a freshman at St. John's and a mother-in-law who's in a nursing home in the Bronx. He was complaining to me just the other day that he's never had serious money trouble in his life—until now."

Very gazed out the window again. "Keep talking."

"Frank was working the hallways at eight o'clock on Halloween night same as George—shooing kids home, encouraging residents to wrap up their parties. Maybe Muriel encountered *him* on her way back to her apartment. Maybe *he* tried to hit her up for a loan, and when she refused, he grabbed her and pulled her into the stairwell. He wore white doorman's gloves, same as George, and wouldn't have worried about leaving fingerprints on the door latch or the bannister. He was well aware that Muriel liked to carry a wad of bucks in her pocketbook. And he's in serious need of bucks, like I said, but . . ."

"But what?"

"I just don't see it. Frank takes a lot of pride in his job. He'd never try to brace a resident for money. It's unprofessional. I also happen to like the guy, as you may have surmised." I tugged at my ear. "Still . . ."

He peered at me. "Still what?"

"When Frank was running through the details of their Halloween security setup for us down in the lobby yesterday, George showed up late for his shift, remember?"

"I remember."

"And Frank was peeved at him, remember?"

"Yeah. He said something about how his wife would already have dinner on the table. So?"

"So I got the feeling that there was something more going on between the two of them. He seemed genuinely pissed at George, which isn't typical of Frank. He's usually a good-natured guy."

Very mulled that over a moment. It was silent in my office. The predawn traffic was very light on Central Park West sixteen floors below. "Are you thinking that maybe he knew that George showed up so late because he'd been to the Dublin House to pay off Choo-Choo?"

"I'm thinking he may know something that we don't know. I'm thinking maybe it's worth having a conversation with him."

"I'm right there with you, dude. Tell you what I'm going to do. I'm going to go home and grab a couple of hours of shut-eye because I'm about ready to drop. And then I'll be back to get you at about nine, nine thirty, unless you need to write."

"I won't be able to write. Not until we settle this. What's your plan?"

"My plan is we keep Raoul in our hip pocket for now. If we need him, we know where to find him. Tomorrow, which is to say today, is Frank's day off. He'll be home raking leaves and storing his patio furniture for the winter, I'm guessing."

"You can always call him if you want to make sure."

Very shook his head at me. "Haven't I taught you *anything* since you stuck your nose into my life? You never, ever tip off a person of interest that you're coming by. You just, *ba-boom*, show up."

"Is that what you'd call Frank—a person of interest?"

"Most definitely. But, as of right now, Bullets still ranks as our prime suspect for gutting George. So our first stop will be Rego Park. And I'm driving."

"In your dreams. We're taking the Jag."

"Not going to happen, dude. This ain't no party. This ain't no disco. This ain't no fooling around. It's a double murder investigation. We'll be arriving in an official vehicle."

"Do you have Bullets under surveillance?"

"What for?"

"Because if he's your prime suspect, he could be halfway to the Canadian border by the time we show up."

"He could be, but he won't be. Bullets isn't going anywhere. He'll just be sitting in a big lounge chair in his living room, waiting for us."

"How do you know that?"

"Dude, how many times do I have to tell you that this is what I do for a living? I *know* it, okay? Now do you have anything else for me? Because I'm about ready to keel over."

"Actually, I do have one more idea, now that you mention it."

Very sighed wearily. "Okay, lay it on me."

So I laid it on him.

I'll say this for Romaine Very—he did know exactly what he was talking about, not that I had doubted him for one second. Bullets Durmond's own living room was exactly where we found Muriel Cantrell's former chauffeur in the morning, seated in a comfy old lounge chair, wearing a burly navy-blue cardigan sweater that looked hand-knit, baggy gray slacks, carpet slippers, and a pair of the reddest, most swollen eyes I'd ever seen. The big man was so utterly grief-stricken that he was there but wasn't there. Didn't so much as acknowledge our presence after we rang the bell and his sister, Rose, ushered us in, her own face etched with worry.

It was a dark, rainy morning with a cold November wind blowing. I wore my trench coat and fedora over the barley tweed suit I'd had made for me in London by Strickland & Sons, a pale-blue shirt, burgundy knit tie, and my Gore-Tex street bluchers. Lulu wore her custom-made duck-billed C. C. Filson rain hat. She's susceptible to sinus problems when she catches colds. Snores like a lumberjack when she has them. I know this because she likes to sleep on my head. Very had picked us up at 9:27. We were waiting for him under the awning out front when he pulled up with a screech, which reminded me that his brakes weren't so hot, either. Merilee had been fast asleep when I'd returned to bed. When I reluctantly got up three hours later to shave, dress, feed Lulu, and down an espresso, she was still out cold, being on Hungarian time. I kissed her on the forehead, stroking her hair gently before I left. She murmured something that sounded vaguely like "woo-tee-ma."

After a bone-jarring, teeth-rattling twenty-minute drive, we crossed the windswept Queensboro Bridge, and Romaine Very worked the battered Crown Vic through the rainy-day traffic on Queens Boulevard. He was unusually pensive and quiet that morning. Asked me nothing. Volunteered no new information. Just drove. He wore a black, hooded rain parka over his usual turtleneck, jeans, and motorcycle boots. Lulu rode between us on the bench seat, her tail thumping happily. She loves to ride in police cars. On rainy days, her protective oily coat gave off a strong scent, not unlike castor oil, that would cling to Very's front seat for, well, ever. But he was so preoccupied he didn't seem to notice.

Rego Park is a solid working-class Queens neighborhood sandwiched in between Elmhurst, notable home of the giant red-and-white-striped Elmhurst gas tanks, and the somewhat more upscale Forest Hills. Bullets lived on Alderton Street, south of Queens Boulevard, north of Woodhaven. The place he shared with Rose was a small, squat one-story redbrick house built in the 1930s, I would guess, with a hip-high chain-link fence and gate surrounding it. A red '87 Buick LeSabre was parked out front. His. Unless red '87 Buick LeSabres were super popular in Rego Park, and who's to say they weren't?

The house seemed even smaller and squatter on the inside. Maybe because of the low ceiling. Maybe because of the two huge people who lived there. Rose was an only slightly scaled-down female version of the big guy—nearly six feet tall and built like a fullback. She had a shock of iron-gray hair, piercing dark eyes, a broad, flat nose, thick lips, and a downturned mouth, the kind that comes from not having smiled for something like thirty-five years. She was a few years older than Bullets, maybe sixty-five, and wore a bulky hand-knit cardigan herself, a large gold cross around her neck, slacks, and carpet slippers. Also a great deal of fruity perfume. Lulu, who is highly allergic to most perfumes, especially fruity ones, started sneezing immediately and stayed put by the front door when Rose gestured for us to join her in the kitchen, which looked as if it hadn't been remodeled since the '50s, back when the whole world was big into yellow. Yellow Formica countertops. Yellow Formica kitchen table. A set of matching chairs with yellow plastic seats and backs. Even the worn linoleum floor was a yellow-and-lime-green floral pattern. It hadn't aged gracefully, in case you're wondering.

The back door, which was double-bolted and chained, led out to a tiny yard where absolutely no soil or member of the plant community appeared to exist. I could make out nothing but bare pavement out there in the pouring rain.

"Sit," Rose commanded us, closing the kitchen door softly. "Coffee?"

We both said, "Please," as we sat at the kitchen table.

She poured us two cups from an electric percolator and put cream, sugar, and a plate of biscotti in front of us before she poured herself a cup and joined us, settling into her chair with a weary sigh. "I got to tell you, when Paulie came home Halloween night and told me that Muriel was gone, I've never seen him so upset in my entire life. He went straight to his room, lay down on the bed with his coat and his shoes still on, and wept and wept, moaning just like a wounded animal. I've been through a lot with him over the years, believe me, but nothing like this. I was so concerned about him that I called Father Mark from our parish, Resurrection-Ascension over on Sixty-First Road, and Father Mark came right over and sat with him. He was so good with him. Didn't say a word. Just sat there and let Paulie talk and talk and talk. We've known Father Mark, must be twenty-seven years now. He's one of the good ones. Really cares about people. Doesn't just stand up there and mouth platitudes at you every Sunday morning, if you know what I mean."

"Did you hear what your brother was saying to him?" Very asked.

"No," she answered abruptly. "I gave him his privacy in case it was, you know, personal."

"Do you mean you thought Father Mark might have been taking his confession?"

"I don't know what I mean," she said, waving Very off with a meaty hand. "I just . . . I stayed here in the kitchen, listened to Jonathan Schwartz play Sinatra on the radio, and made biscotti. Yesterday morning I convinced Paulie to shower, shave, and put on fresh clothes. But I couldn't get him to say a word to me or eat a thing. He just sat there in his chair in the living room and sobbed all day. Father Mark came back in the late afternoon and sat with him again for hours. Well past midnight."

"Was he here with your brother this morning at two a.m.?"

She peered at Very guardedly. "Yeah. Why you asking?"

"And he'll confirm that?"

"Of course he will. Why you asking?" she repeated.

Very didn't respond for a moment, no doubt because he was thinking exactly what I was thinking. If Bullets was here in Rego Park with his priest at two in the morning, sobbing, then he couldn't have been on West Eighty-Second Street gutting George with a carving knife. "Just making conversation," he answered finally.

"Just making conversation my Aunt Fanny," Rose snarled at him. "You think Paulie did something, don't you? Well, you can forget that. He didn't. He was right here, and Father Mark will tell you so. And if you think Father Mark would tell a lie to protect Paulie, he'd never do that. He's one of the good ones."

"So you said."

"What's *that* supposed to mean?" she demanded, glaring at him.

"I was just agreeing with you," Very said.

"Like hell you were."

Very refused to get into an argument with her. Just sipped his coffee calmly. "You were saying Father Mark stayed and sat with your brother for hours."

"Without so much as glancing at his watch," she said, continuing to glare at him. "He was here for Paulie for as long as Paulie needed him. I heated up some lasagna so the poor man wouldn't starve. When Paulie finally dozed off in his chair at around two, Father Mark quietly let himself out. But he's already called me twice this morning to see how Paulie's doing—which you two can see with your own eyes."

"He's not himself," I said. "It's as if he's in a daze."

She raised her chin at me. "*You* with your tall, lanky build and fair coloring I can tell are a Protestant of some kind," she said, her voice dripping with distaste. "But Romaine Very . . . that's a Catholic name, isn't it?"

"My parents practice. I don't."

She looked at him with great concern. "You don't have God in your life?"

"After what I've seen on this job, it's hard to believe that there is a God."

"That's no way to talk." She studied him over the rim of her coffee cup. "So you're the great Romaine Very. I've read about you in the newspaper. You're much younger than I thought you'd be. Better looking, too."

"You're not hitting on me, are you, Rose?" he asked her teasingly.

She rolled her eyes. "Oh, please. My shenanigan days are long gone. I'm a fat, sixty-six-year-old spinster. I worked at a stationery store on Woodhaven Boulevard for years until Staples put them out of business. Now I keep house for my kid brother and go to church. Not much of a life, is it?"

"Doesn't sound so bad to me."

"Is that right? Try trading places with me."

"I didn't realize your brother was a devout Catholic."

"It's how we were raised. Our parents were working people. They left us nothing but this house and their faith. Paulie never got very far in school. He had trouble concentrating. He made a living the only way he knew how—by being tough and doing what he was told, even if it meant that he had to leave me all alone here for years at a stretch." She narrowed her piercing eyes at him. "But you'd know all about that, wouldn't you?"

"His record's not exactly a secret. You don't happen to have a carving knife missing from a drawer in here, do you, Rose?"

"What kind of question is that?" she demanded angrily.

"The kind I don't want to ask but have to, trust me."

"I *don't* trust you. I was raised to believe that all cops are on the take. You know why? Because they are. I've been around a long time, and if there's one thing I know, it's that no one moves up the ladder as fast as you have without being a crooked weasel," she said fiercely, sounding exactly like who she was—the big sister of a lifelong mob enforcer.

"I'm sorry you feel that way."

"I don't want your sorrow," she said roughly. "I got no use for it. And if you want to have a look at my kitchen knives go right ahead—*after* you get a search warrant."

Very drained his coffee and went to work on a fresh piece of bubble gum, changing his tone of voice to match hers. "We're going to have a talk with him now."

"Go ahead and try," she said.

"Will you be joining us?"

"What, and help you milk him for information? Not a chance. No, I'll stay right here. But he's very upset. If you so much as *try* to get tricky with him, you'll have me to answer to."

Very let that particular remark slide on by. He knew better than to tangle with her. Just thanked her for the coffee, got to his feet, and went into the living room. We both did.

It was the kind of living room that had plastic slip-covers over the sofa and lampshades. A chair from the dining room had been pulled over next to Bullets's big lounge chair. Father Mark's chair, I gathered. I grabbed another one from the dining room, and Very and I sat there with him. Bullets seemed a million miles from nowhere. Didn't acknowledge our presence. Just gazed off into space with his red, swollen eyes, his breath wheezing in and out through his smashed nose. It felt claustrophobic in there. Smelled like musty carpeting, with a hint of mothballs, Bengay, denture cleanser, reheated lasagna, and Rose's fruity perfume. There was also a faint hint of castor oil coming from Lulu's rain-dampened coat. She remained stretched out by the front door with her duck-billed cap on and her face buried between her paws, sniffling from Rose's perfume. I thought about putting her in Very's car, but it would be awfully cold and damp out there. She'd be better off in the house.

"Hey, Bullets," Very said in a soothing voice. "How's it going?"

The big man blinked, stirring from his daze. Looked at Very blankly, then at me with a faint hint of recognition.

"Where's your little d-dog?" he asked me hoarsely. "Where's Lulu?"

"She's right over there by the door. Doesn't care for Rose's perfume."

"Find m-me someone who does. Doesn't stop Rose from wearing it." Bullets spotted Lulu at the door and smiled faintly. "Hey, Lulu," he called to her. "Hey, g-girl."

She thudded her tail in response.

"Did Rose g-give you some coffee, Lieutenant? It's Lieutenant Very, right?"

"It is. And she did," Very said.

"How about something to eat? She's a hell of a c-cook."

"We're good, thanks."

He ran a giant hand over his battle-scarred face. "Please excuse me. These have b-been the toughest two nights of m-my whole life. Even tougher than when they locked that cell door behind me in Rahway b-back when I-I took my first fall." He gazed at me and said, "Did you ever love someone not j-just to say the words, but really, truly love her? I mean, way d-deep down inside?"

"Yes, I have," I said. "Still do."

"I never had b-before," he said to me. He seemed to have forgotten about Very for the moment. "Not once in m-my whole life. But Muriel, w-we were together for twelve good, long years and, God, I-I loved her. Not the way you're thinking, like I wanted to g-get naked with her or such . . ."

I shuddered inwardly at the thought of seeing Bullets Durmond naked. Over by the door, Lulu let out a low, unhappy moan of her own.

Bullets frowned at her. "She okay?"

"Fine. She just makes odd noises sometimes. Pay no attention."

"Muriel was the k-kindest, most caring person I've ever known. I never felt so close to nobody else. The two of us, we were t-together in that Silver Cloud four, five times a week for all of those years just like an old m-married couple, she used to kid me. I could tell her anything. And she c-could tell me anything. We laughed together. Sometimes we even c-cried together. Being with her, that was my whole world. I told Father Mark it w-was the closest I can imagine to w-what having a wife would be like. I n-never got lucky that way. Al Pacino I'm n-not. From the t-time I was sixteen the girls got one look at me and ran. Muriel, she n-never made me feel like a freak. She was good to me. I-I trusted her and . . . *loved* her. When you g-get to be in your sixties like I am, and don't have that many years left, you know you're never g-going to love anybody else that way again. Not ever. That's a t-tough pill to swallow. 'A small death of its own.' That's what Father

Mark c-called it. I c-can't imagine how I'll go on. What's the point? What have I got t-to look forward to? You're a smart guy, Hoagy. Tell me, will ya? Gimme an answer."

I didn't have an answer for him. There wasn't one.

He turned to look at Very now. "Who d-did it?" he demanded. "Who killed my Muriel?"

"We don't know yet. There's a new wrinkle to the case that I'm figuring you don't know about yet. Not unless you got a call early this morning from Frank or Harvey."

"I haven't g-gotten no calls from nobody." Bullets peered at him in confusion. "What kind of new wrinkle?"

"George Strull was knifed to death outside of his apartment on West Eighty-Second just after two a.m. when he got off of his shift."

Bullets continued to peer at him in confusion. "George *who*?"

"The night man at Muriel's building."

"You m-mean her doorman?"

"That's right."

"He's . . . dead, you said?"

"Don't get any deader. But you're in the clear if Father Mark backs Rose's story that he was right here with you when George's murder went down."

"I could have t-told you that myself," Bullets said defensively.

"You could have," Very acknowledged. "But it means a lot more if someone else, someone like an ordained priest, can back you up—especially considering you've served time for involuntary manslaughter and assault and battery. Plus I understand you broke three of George's ribs a while back."

Bullets sat there for a moment, wheezing in and out, before he said, "The bastard was asking me questions about where Muriel's money c-came from. It was none of his d-damned business. He was her freaking doorman, that's all. Also a d-drinker with a gambling problem. So I d-discouraged him from asking any more questions about her."

"That's all there was to it?" Very asked.

"That's all. And now he's dead, hunh? So who stuck him?"

The kitchen door opened and Rose, who apparently was unable to stop herself, came in with a fresh percolator of coffee and a tray with cups and a plate of biscotti. She set it on the coffee table. "They giving you a hard time?" she asked her brother in a gentle voice.

"Naw. Came t-to talk to me about George."

"George who?"

"Doorman at Muriel's building."

"What about him?"

231

"Somebody stuck a-a knife in him at two in the morning."

Rose immediately shot a dirty look at Very.

Bullets gestured at her with his chin. "Go b-back in the kitchen, will you? Leave us alone."

She left us alone, but not before shooting another dirty look Very's way.

"Rose doesn't like me," he said to Bullets.

"Rose doesn't like anyone. Why d-do you think she never found a husband?" He reached for a biscotti, munching on it. "So you d-don't know who stuck him, do you?"

"We don't know," Very conceded. "But we do know that he paid his bookie, Choo-Choo, two grand in crisp, new hundred-dollar bills at the Dublin House before he showed up for his shift yesterday."

"Where'd he c-come into dough like that?" Bullets asked.

"Excellent question. Our crime scene technicians said that whoever shoved Muriel down those stairs didn't bother to wipe down the bannister or the hallway door latches."

Bullets gazed at him blankly. "You lost me there. What does that m-mean?"

"It means that maybe her killer wore gloves. Doormen wear gloves. And George, with his serious gambling problem, had serious money trouble. We figure he tried to hit Muriel up for money when she was returning to her apartment from Alan Levin's Halloween party."

"No way she'd give him a n-nickel," Bullets scoffed.

"Exactly. And when she told him to get lost, he pulled her into the stairwell and demanded she hand over her pocketbook. Maybe she tripped and fell. Maybe he shoved her. We don't know. A complete autopsy may give us an indication. But either way she ended up dead, her pocketbook ended up missing, and George suddenly produced two grand that he owed to his bookie."

"If I'd known h-he was responsible I wouldn't have used n-no knife on him, I'll tell you that much." Bullets' eyes turned into furious slits as he sat there, clenching and unclenching his huge fists. "I would have used these."

"Well, someone got to him before you did. Any idea who it might have been?"

Bullets blinked at Very in surprise. "How w-would I know?"

"You logged a lot of hours on the sofa in that lobby. You heard things, saw things. Did anyone have it in for George?"

The big man mulled it over, shifting his bulk in the lounge chair. "Can't help you. All I can tell you is he w-wasn't a friendly guy. Never had a-a smile on his face.

Not like Frank. Frank's always b-been nice to me. We'd t-talk sports when no one else was around. He's a big Mets fan, same as me." Bullets fell silent, his chin dipping to his chest. "I don't know what I'm g-going to do with myself now," he said mournfully.

"Give it some time," I said. "I know it seems impossible to believe right now, but the pain will subside. When it does, give Sandy Panisch, Muriel's Jewish lawyer, a call."

"Why would I want to d-do that?"

"Because Muriel made a special provision for you in her will."

"What k-kind of provision?"

"She left you the Silver Cloud. It'll be yours now."

"*Mine*? I can't believe she'd . . ." His mouth tightened, his eyes tearing up. "I'd never be able to drive it. It'd bring b-back too many memories. Make me sad."

"I suspect she knew that."

"Then why'd she leave it t-to me?"

"As a severance package. She wanted to make sure you'd be comfortable in your old age."

"Don't kid me. This *is* my old age."

I dug my card from my wallet and handed it to him. "When you're ready, I can put you in touch with a terrific antique car broker in East Hampton. He's the fellow whom Merilee and I got the Jag from. He'll make sure you get top dollar for it. Just do me one small favor. Don't let him sell it to Gary and Olivia Pennington Kates, okay?"

Bullets let out something vaguely akin to a chuckle, although it sounded more like he had a chicken bone stuck in his throat. "Sure thing, pal."

"Unless I'm wrong, and I'm not, that Silver Cloud will fetch enough so that you and Rose can buy yourselves a nice two-bedroom winter condo down in Boca."

"I hate Florida. They have c-crocodiles down there."

"Alligators."

"Them, too." He turned to Very and said, "You'll c-call me, right? When you figure out what happened to her?"

"I'll call you," Very promised.

Bullets turned back to me again, smiling faintly. "Muriel liked you. Thought you were a-a gentleman. Real class. And that you were gifted. That was the word she used. Gifted. She was real sorry that you have your d-demons, or w-whatever they are."

"I didn't pick an easy career to go into."

"We don't pick 'em. They pick us. Muriel used to tell me that Miss Nash was a much happier person b-back when you two were together. And that she just wasn't the same a-after you split up. She did date other men . . ."

"She even married one briefly. That fabulously successful playwright, Zach somebody."

"But n-never had that same glow she had when you were living there. Muriel was real g-glad that you two got back together. 'The glow is back.' That's how she p-put it to me."

"Thanks for sharing that with me. I'm kind of glad myself." I heard a disgruntled cough from over by the front door. "And I'm not the only one."

"I wonder . . . I mean, d-do you think it made Muriel happy that *I* was around?"

"Bullets, I don't doubt it for one second."

"Whoa, was that a genuine house of unearthly delights or what?" Very jabbered at me as he went tearing away from the little brick place on Alderton Street and hung a screeching left onto Queens Boulevard. The rain had let up. A biting November wind was blowing. Not that Lulu cared. She still stood in my lap with her head stuck out the window, the better to rid the residue of Rose's fruity perfume from her large, wet black nose. "And, dude, talk about claustrophobic. I kept feeling like I was going to suffocate, know what I'm saying?"

"I absolutely do. I had the same feeling. For one thing, it felt as if time had stopped there in 1957, which totally creeped me out. But the worst part was sitting in that stuffy living room listening to Bullets unload his lifetime of emotional hurt."

"I hear you. Made me want to lie down with a cold cloth over my head." Very glanced over at me. "You were good with him. Sympathetic."

"I've taken a strange liking to Bullets, to be perfectly honest."

"Just between us, so have I. Not that I should. He's a mob enforcer who's taken two falls and done away with God knows how many enemies. But he's old school. Honest, loyal. There aren't too many of his sort still around. The new crowd's a bunch of coked-out wild animals. And you for damned sure won't catch one of them taking his big sister to Mass on Sunday."

As we hightailed our way along Queens Boulevard, bouncing in and out of every pothole, we bid a wistful farewell to Rego Park and said hello to scenic Elmhurst, zipping our way past one used-car lot and fast-food franchise after another after another.

"Are you going to check out his alibi with Father Mark?" I asked Very.

"If I have to. And I sincerely hope I don't."

"Why's that?"

"Because if Bullets told him anything self-incriminating while Father Mark was in the process of taking his confession, then Father Mark will refuse to give me a straight answer. It'll get super awkward. It's no fun to question a priest, believe me."

"I believe you."

"Especially if you're Catholic yourself."

"Yeah, I was able to glean that from your remark."

"There's another one, dude. *Glean*. I never get to hear that word. It's a good word."

"I've always been fond of it."

He glanced over at me, his head nodding, nodding. "Want to know what's driving me crazy about this case?"

"Do tell."

"Every single indicator points to Bullets as George's killer. In fact, it's a slam dunk, whether Father Mark backs his alibi or not. Not once have I come up against an alibi that I couldn't poke a hole in. I'm not bragging, just speaking the real. The most likely scenario is that Bullets heard on the grapevine that George laid two grand in crisp hundreds on Choo-Choo yesterday afternoon. Bullets put two and two together, which I believe he's more than capable of doing, and figured there's only one way George could have gotten his hands on that kind of dough. So he showed up at George's place when George got off of his shift and took care of business. Did the job he was being paid to do for the past twelve years. He was supposed to be Muriel's protector, after all, and he let her down and felt like shit about it. It all adds up, except for the part where every instinct I possess tells me that he's not our killer. Did you notice the way Rose immediately jumped to the conclusion that he was? She got super defensive with all of that 'Get a warrant' stuff. Pattern of a lifetime for her. But, being honest? Sitting there with him, I just didn't feel it."

"I didn't feel it either."

"So it's not just me?"

"No, it's not just you. So where does that leave us?"

"Where does that leave us?" Very's jaw muscles clenched. "Good question."

"Thank you, Lieutenant. I try to ask good questions. It's one of the reasons I'm in such high demand as a celebrity ghostwriter. A lot of the lunch-pail ghosts just go through the motions. Ask standard press-kit questions. Settle for pat answers. Don't keep after their celebrity to come up with something that's unexpected and more insightful and—"

"You can shut the hell up any time you feel like it."

So I shut the hell up. I knew his outburst was nothing personal. He was upset. He also suffers from an intensity issue, which is to say he has too much of it.

By now we'd waved goodbye to Elmhurst and were now in the venerable Irish American, working-class enclave of Woodside. Very hung a screeching right at Roosevelt Avenue and worked his way to Fifty-Fourth Street, which was made up of aging, semidetached wood-framed and brick houses. It was quiet there on a weekday morning. The kids were in school. The men were at work. A couple of fifty-something housewives were walking slowly along the wet sidewalk, pushing grocery carts. It seemed dreary and depressing there under the gray November sky with the wind blowing. Or maybe it was just the mood I was in.

Very slowed up as he checked out the house numbers. Pulled up in front of our destination, 41-51, which happened to be the narrow, two-story semidetached home of Francis O'Brien, better known as Frank the doorman. It was a wood-framed house that looked as if it had been built back around the turn of the century and was getting tired. It seemed to sag in the middle. Its pea-soup-green paint was peeling, and Frank had told me that it needed a new roof. Downstairs, the narrow house was only two windows and a front door wide. Upstairs it had three windows. There were two window air conditioners, one downstairs, the other upstairs. It had a shallow front yard with a couple of scraggly bushes and a hip-high chain-link fence around it. You never see hip-high chain-link fences in Manhattan. I'd been in Queens for less than a full morning and I'd already seen two.

I put Lulu's duck-billed cap back on her head in case the rain decided to stage a comeback, and we got out. Very knocked on Frank's aluminum screen door, which was dented in several places and didn't exactly hang straight. When no one answered, he opened the screen door and pounded on the wooden front door. Still no answer. There was a narrow driveway adjacent to the house that led back to a two-car garage. The garage door was open. A blue Dodge Ram pickup, maybe five years old, was parked in one of the spaces. The other space was empty. The driveway had an apron back there so that they could turn around when they pulled out of the garage and leave nose first instead of having to back all the way down to the street. There was a patio, a small patch of weedy lawn, and zero privacy. The redbrick house adjacent to the driveway had windows that looked directly out over Frank's patio and weedy lawn.

We found him wiping down his rain-soaked patio chairs and stowing them in the basement. There was a pair of aluminum Bilco doors adjacent to the back door that he'd flung open wide. A short flight of concrete steps led down to the basement. Frank wore a St. John's hooded sweatshirt, jeans, and work boots. Once again, I noticed how he came across like a completely different person when he was out of uniform. Less dignified. Less commanding. Just a guy.

"Well, hey, fellas," he said in surprise when he saw us, wiping his wet hands on a towel. "What brings you two high rollers out here to paradise?" On Lulu's low moan he added, "Excuse me, you *three* high rollers." Before either of us could respond, Frank's cheery, apple-cheeked face dropped. "Oh, hey, this must be about George."

Very's jaw went to work on a fresh piece of bubble gum. "Afraid so."

"Raoul called me about it first thing this morning," Frank said grimly.

"Do you mind talking about George for a minute?"

"Heck, no. Not at all. I was never really a big fan of the guy, to be honest, but he sure didn't deserve getting a knife in the gut." Frank swiped at some mud on the knees of his jeans. "You know, it never fails. I always fall behind on my seasonal chores, and the *one* day I finally set aside to take care of everything, it pours. After I fold that patio table and stow it in the garage, I've got to pull the air conditioners out of the windows and horse them down to the basement. God, I hate that job. Kills my back every time." He stood there, hands on his hips, gazing up at the back of the house. "Not much, is it? I meant to take a power sander to it this summer and put on a fresh coat of paint. Just never seemed to get around to it—maybe because I can always find something better to do than spending all day on a ladder. The realtor called this a handyman's special when we bought it back in '79. It's still a handyman's special. The plumbing's no good. The wiring's no good. And I'll let you in on a little secret. I'm nobody's idea of a handyman. I was hoping Frank Jr. would give me a hand this summer, but he made St. John's football team as a walk-on and had to be at practice every day. He's a big, husky kid. They think they can make an offensive lineman out of him. Did either of you ever play?"

"In a manner of speaking," I said. "I was our punter my sophomore year. But track was my main sport."

Frank tilted his head at me appraisingly. "You're built like a . . . hurdler, am I right?"

"Actually, I was a spear chucker. Third best in the entire Ivy League."

"No kidding. All these years and I never knew that. It's funny the things you find out about people when you're in different surroundings. Hey, I'm not being much of a host. Buy you guys a beer?"

I declined. Very shook his head.

"Yeah, I guess it's a little early in the day. And you want to talk to me about George, not listen to me rattle on. Sure thing," he said as he watched Lulu sniff her way idly around the yard. "I doubt there's much I can tell you that you don't already know. He was a gloomy, bitter guy

243

who drank and gambled. His wife dumped him and took up with another man, and George was practically living out of a suitcase in that illegal sublet Raoul found for him. Being honest, he wasn't my idea of a reliable coworker. Showed up late for his shift all the time, sometimes with liquor on his breath. I'd have to cover for him, which meant I'd get home late for dinner and, boy, would I hear about it from Sharon."

"You seemed pretty upset with him the other day," I said.

"Damned straight I was. He was a whole hour late."

Very studied him, jaw working on his gum, before he glanced over at the garage and said, "Where's your beater?"

Frank shook his head. "Sorry, my what?"

"Your white '84 Chevy Caprice," Very said, turning to look at me. "That was an awesome lead you laid on me in your office, dude. Especially considering it was four thirty a.m. Frank does indeed own a Chevy. Mind you, my people would have found out within the next twenty-four to forty-eight hours as part of their routine background check. But, thanks to you, I turned it up this morning before I picked you up. I sure do admire the way your mind works, and there aren't many people who I can say that about. There's Norma, there's Frank Zappa, there's you . . ." He turned back to Frank. "Where'd you say it was?"

"I didn't," Frank responded. "Sharon has it. Had to take my sister to an appointment with her surgeon this morning." He scratched his head. "I must admit I'm a little confused here, Lieutenant."

Very let out a laugh. "Now you're living in my world."

"Why do you care what kind of car I drive?"

"That old Caprice has a V-8 under its hood, doesn't it?"

Frank nodded miserably. "Total gas guzzler. Gets, I swear, eight miles to a gallon."

"Plus it needs a new muffler, correct?"

Frank gaped at him in amazement. "Now how on earth did you know that?"

"Neighbor who was awake in bed directly across the street from George's building heard what sounded like a Chevy V-8 in need of a new muffler idling out there right around the time that someone was gutting George with a carving knife."

Frank let out a chuckle. "What is this guy, a mechanic?"

"No, she's an assistant editor at *Vogue*, actually. She said someone got out of the car, then got back in a couple of minutes later and drove away at about two thirty a.m." Very paused for a moment before he said, "Where were you at two thirty?"

"Right here in bed. Where the heck else would I be? I'm not exactly a late-night partier." He wasn't exactly as cheery as he'd been a few minutes ago, either. Tense was more like it. He made his way over to the aluminum patio table, wiped it down with the towel, turned it on its side, and folded up its legs. When he was done, the table was as flat as a door. He propped it against the side of the garage, his movements not exactly smooth and natural. Slow and stiff was more like it.

"I've been on the job for a while now, Frank," Very said. "Not to puff myself up, but I'm good at what I do. So when I tell you what I'm about to tell you, I want you to listen to me extremely carefully, okay?"

Frank cleared his throat. "Sure, okay . . ."

"This whole case is about to land on you like an anvil. You're a decent guy. A family man, union man, hard worker. You have no sheet. Not even a parking ticket. So here's the thing, here's the thing—I'm going to do you a solid and tell you what the smart move is."

Frank gazed at him in confusion. "The smart move?"

"Tell us how it went down while it's just us three talking. No one else is here. No tape recorder is rolling. No one from the DA's office is writing anything down. Get out in front of it—and I mean right now."

"But what makes you think that *I* know anything?" Frank wondered.

"Because you do. You're the only one who does. Not Bullets. Not Raoul. Not Harvey. Not Trevor the tweaker. Not Muriel's old friend Myrna. Or her lawyer, Sandy Panisch. Or any of her neighbors. Not Gary and Olivia. Not Alan and Gretchen. And for sure not Hoagy and Merilee. So just tell us how it went down. Do that and I'll do everything within my power to help you. You have my word. And I keep my word. Go ahead and ask Hoagy."

"The Lieutenant's talking to you straight, Frank," I said. "You can trust him. And he has friends in high places."

Frank scratched his head again. "Boy, am I confused. I'd sure like to help you out, Lieutenant. Really, I would. But I have absolutely no idea what you're talking about."

"Okay, playing dumb's *not* the smart move," Very said, turning brusque. "That will get you nowhere. Try a do-over. And I don't have all day, Frank."

Frank stood there in uneasy silence for a long moment, his wheels spinning, before he finally said, "I wonder if maybe I should call a lawyer."

"That's certainly one way to play it," Very acknowledged. "But it's not the smart way. Frank, I'm giving you one more chance and then I'm slamming the door shut. Where were you at two thirty this morning?"

Frank took a deep, ragged breath, letting it out slowly before he sat down on the damp pavement, resting his back against the folded patio table. "Okay, sure. I . . . I wasn't home in bed."

"Now we're getting somewhere," Very said approvingly. "That's an excellent start. Here's what I want you to do for me now. I want you to hit rewind to Halloween night. It's eight o'clock. Harvey's on the front door. You, George, and Raoul are working the building, floor by floor, asking folks to wrap up their open house parties. Checking the service stairs for any kids who need shooing home. Tell us what happened to Muriel."

"I don't know, Lieutenant."

Very let out a huge sigh of disappointment. "Damn, and we were doing so good there for a second, Frank." He shook his head at me. "You can't say I didn't give him a fair shot, can you, dude?"

"You gave him as fair a shot as you could. No question about it."

"Okay, I'm afraid that this means we're done here, Frank. On your feet. I have to take you in for official questioning. Let's go."

"What I meant to say," Frank added hurriedly, his voice quavering, "is that I don't know *exactly* what happened. And that's the God's honest truth. I only know what I saw and, um, what George told me."

Very's jaw worked on his bubble gum. "Keep talking."

Frank sat there in taut silence for a moment, breathing in and out, before he said, "I was making my rounds, like you said, when I opened the door to the fifteenth-floor service stairs and let out a gasp—George was standing right there on the landing over Muriel, who was lying on the floor staring straight at me, dead as dead can be. Her face was caved in. Her neck was twisted all out of whack. *Sideways.* She looked like a broken doll. And George, who had her pocketbook in his hand, had the guiltiest look on his face I'd ever seen. 'I didn't push her, Frank,' he said to me. 'She tripped, I swear.' That's what I meant when I told you I don't know what happened, Lieutenant. Because I don't. I didn't see it happen with my own two eyes. I only know what George told me. I said to him, 'Why on earth was Muriel in the stairwell?' And he said, 'I was just asking her for a favor, that's all.' So I said, 'Are you telling me you dragged that nice little old lady in here to hit her up for money?' And he said, 'I'm in real trouble, Frank. Choo-Choo's going to break both of my legs if I don't come up with two grand by tomorrow. Only, she wouldn't loan it to me. Got all huffy. She was a mean old bitch. Cheap, too. She would *not* let go of her damned pocketbook. Wrestled me for it, can you believe it? That's when she tripped and fell.'" Frank trailed off, his face scrunching with emotion. "Then George opened the pocketbook and yanked out a thick wad of hundred-dollar bills. 'There must be four, five grand here, Frank,' he said. 'I'll split it with you if you keep quiet, okay? You got money troubles of your own, right? So take it. Nobody ever has to know. It'll be our secret. Just between the two of us.'"

"So what did you say to him?" Very asked Frank, who had a look of utter misery on his face as he sat there on the pavement, his back resting against the folded table.

"I'm a law-abiding citizen, Lieutenant. I wanted nothing to do with Muriel's money. And I for sure didn't want an unreliable drunk like George Strull as a partner in crime. Hell, he'd be able to hold it over me forever. Hit me up for money whenever he needed it. And I didn't doubt for one second that if the shit ever hit the fan, he'd tell the cops that *I* was the one who killed her."

"So what did you say to him?" Very repeated, louder this time.

"I said, 'George, I didn't see anything and I didn't hear anything. Your secret's safe with me. And I don't want a penny of that money. It's all yours.' He stared at me in total amazement and said, 'You sure about this, Frank?' And I said, 'Positive.' So George scurried off with the pocketbook and I went on about my business, and a few minutes later Raoul found her there."

"That would explain why George kicked Lulu when we were all down in the lobby," I said. "He was afraid she'd recognize Muriel's scent on him and raise a fuss. Besides, I didn't buy that story of his about how he'd been bit by a rabid dog when he was a kid. It sounded made up."

Frank nodded. "Because it was."

"Forgive me if I sound a tad dense here, Frank, but I don't understand why you didn't turn George in to Lieutenant Very right there on the spot."

"That doesn't surprise me," Frank responded with a hint of defiance in his voice. "You wouldn't understand. Neither one of you. You're both Ivy Leaguers. Raised in nice neighborhoods, good homes. And your fathers taught you to be good little gentlemen, too, am I right? Well, that's not how my old man raised me. And it's not how George's old man raised him. Oh, sure, I have good manners. And I look real dignified in my uniform. But I'm not like you at all. I was schooled by the rules of the street, and you don't rat out one of your own. Not a neighbor, not a union brother, nobody—even if you don't like the guy. And I didn't like George. He was a no-good louse. But if you've got a problem with somebody, you take care of it yourself. You don't go crying for help. You sure as hell don't go to the cops, who aren't to be trusted."

A less than friendly attitude toward the police seemed to be a running theme that morning. "You aren't by any chance friends with Rose Durmond, are you?" I asked him.

"Rose *who*?"

"Never mind. You were saying . . ."

"Those are the rules I was taught to live by. George shoved that sweet old lady down those stairs. Hell, he looked so damned guilty standing over her I *knew* he killed her. But I handled it the way I was taught to. I took care of it myself. Not that it was an easy choice, believe me. I stewed and stewed about it. Couldn't sleep a wink last night. Just lay there staring at the ceiling with my stomach in knots. But I knew what I had to do. So I got up, got dressed, and—"

"Wait, what did you tell Sharon?" Very interjected.

Frank lowered his eyes uncomfortably. "That part was no problem. I've been sleeping on the living room sofa for weeks. Things have been on the rocky side between us since my sister moved in. Those two have never gotten along, and Sharon feels like I dumped her in her lap. Which I guess I did. But she's my sister. She's broke. She's sick. What was I supposed to do, abandon her? Believe me, she gets on my nerves, too. But it's Sharon who has to drive her to her doctor appointments and listen to her bitch and moan all day while I'm off working in my nice, fancy building on Central Park West. It, um, it isn't exactly like *Ozzie and Harriet* around here."

I said, "Trust me, it isn't like *Ozzie and Harriet* anywhere. Ozzie Nelson has a lot to answer for."

"When I finished getting dressed, I went in the kitchen and grabbed a carving knife from the drawer. We had three. Wedding presents. Now we have two. I figured she'd never notice if one was missing. I'm the one who carves the turkey at Thanksgiving. Then I slipped out the back door, jumped in the Chevy, and took off."

"Sharon didn't hear you drive away?"

Frank shook his head. "Our bedroom's in the front, and she's a sound sleeper. Didn't say a word to me about it this morning. Besides, I was gone less than two hours. Back under the covers in the living room when she came downstairs to put the coffee on."

"So talk us through it," Very said. "You drove to West Eighty-Second Street and were sitting there, idling in your car, when George came home from work. He unlocked the door to his apartment and . . . ?"

"And there I was, right in his face."

"Was he shocked to see you?"

"He barely had time to react at all. I stuck him as soon as I saw him. No dawdling. And for damned sure no conversation. I was wearing a pair of work gloves. I slammed

253

him against the doorjamb, planted my left hand over his mouth and stuck him deep in the gut—deep enough I was sure he wouldn't live to talk about it. Then I got back in the car and drove home. Tossed the work gloves out the window on my way. When I got home, I came in the back door and checked myself over in the powder room to see if I had any blood on me. Which I didn't. Not so much as a spot on my face, my jacket, anywhere. Then I washed my hands, got undressed, and climbed back under the covers, like I told you."

"I'm curious," I said. "How did it feel when you were lying there on the sofa, knowing what you'd just done?"

Frank had to mull that one over for a moment. "I didn't feel guilty or tormented, if that's what you're wondering. George needed to pay for what he did to Muriel. And he paid. I felt like I . . . I felt like I did what my dad would have expected me to do, I guess. I did what needed to be done, and I took pride in that. I was asleep in no time. And that's the whole story, guys. I really don't have anything else to tell you. Except for one thing . . ."

Very studied him. "Which is . . . ?"

"That it's amazing how fast your life can turn to crap."

"Boggles the mind," I agreed.

Frank climbed slowly to his feet, groaning from some stiffness in his back, and picked up the folded patio table he'd been leaning against. "I'm going to move this to the back wall of the garage if you don't mind."

"Naw, go ahead," Very said. "Need help with it?"

"Not necessary, Lieutenant. It's just cheapo aluminum. Doesn't weigh a thing." It was no trouble at all for a big, strapping guy like Frank to carry it to the back wall behind his Dodge Ram and prop it there. As we stood in the apron of his driveway, watching him, he suddenly reached inside the rolled-down window of his truck and grabbed something from the front seat.

Something that was a Smith & Wesson .38 revolver.

CHAPTER EIGHT

We'd underestimated Frank.

He'd been expecting us.

He was ready for us—and fired two shots at us so quickly that neither one of us had time to react.

The first shot went high and wide.

The second smacked into Very's left thigh. Very let out a groan of pain and crumpled to the ground.

I grabbed him by the shoulders and dragged him the ten feet or so to the open cellar doors. Frank fired off a third shot that pinged off one of the doors as we dove headfirst down the cellar steps with Lulu right along with us.

Very pulled his SIG and peered outside from the top step. Right away, another shot pinged off one of the cellar doors. "No good, he's hiding behind . . . the . . . the truck," Very started breathing heavily as he tumbled his way back down the steps to the cellar floor. He had a look at his blood-drenched jeans. "Damn, it's a bleeder, dude," he gasped. "Hit my femoral artery. My heart's pumping all the blood in my body right out of me. I'll bleed out in, like, five minutes if you don't tie me off." He looked as if he might pass out sooner than that. He was turning deathly pale. "Need a tourniquet. And, shit, I'm not wearing a belt."

"Not to worry, Lieutenant. You'll be happy to know I never made the transish to Continental slacks," I said, keeping my voice calm as I rapidly unbuckled my belt and yanked it out of its loops. It was a cherished favorite that Grandfather had bought for himself in Venice on his honeymoon. But now was no time for sentiment. "Just hang in there. I've got your back." I began wrapping it tightly around his thigh, where the blood was literally spurting from the gunshot wound.

"You're . . . a good friend."

"Not going to get sloppy and sentimental on me, are you?" I wrapped the belt around his thigh as tight as I could and secured it with a figure-eight knot, yanking hard on it.

"Harder . . . !" he groaned.

That was when Lulu nudged me aside, pressed her front paws against the outside of Very's thigh, grabbed the knot in her powerful jaws, and yanked it toward her with every ounce of strength in her fifty-pound body, a low growl coming from her throat. The two of us have gotten ourselves into a lot of jams over the years, yet she never ceases to amaze me with her survival instincts.

"Better?" I asked him.

"Better . . . Jeez, she's strong."

"I don't just keep her around for her looks. Haven't you figured that out by now?" I wriggled my way up the top step and spotted two of Frank's neighbors peering out the windows of the two-story brick house next door. "WE'VE GOT A POLICE OFFICER DOWN!" I hollered to them at the top of my lungs. "CALL 911! WE NEED AN AMBU-LANCE NOW! A POLICEMAN'S BEEN SHOT!"

The two heads disappeared from the windows just as Frank fired at me, the shot nicking the top step less than a foot from me. I ducked back down.

"Here, dude . . ." Very gasped, as Lulu continued to tug on the tourniquet, her front paws getting soaked with his blood. "Take my SIG."

I took it from him. "I'm not going to shoot him, Lieutenant."

He didn't respond. He'd faded on me for a second, his eyes rolling back before they fluttered back into focus again.

I could hear sirens way off in the distance now, heading our way at high speed. More than one. Sounded like at least two, maybe three. "Hear that? The cavalry's coming. Just hang on," I implored him, gripping his hand as Lulu continued to pull with all her might on Grandfather's favorite belt.

"He'll be . . . long gone by the time they get here," Very told me, panting for breath. "He's working up the nerve to make a run for it. You've got to take him. Ever fire a SIG before?"

I crouched there, holding it in my hand. "Not exactly."

"Have you ever fired a *gun* before?"

"Does Old Betsy count?"

"Old *who*?"

"My Davy Crockett cap rifle when I was a kid."

"Uh . . . yeah. Same idea. Just point it and . . ." His eyes rolled back in his head again as he started to lose consciousness.

"Listen to me!" I shook him by the arms. "Are you listening? There's something I've got to get off my chest. I fucked Norma before she took up with you."

He blinked at me. "You *what*?"

"It's true. Merilee was in Budapest, and when Norma edits a writer, she's *all* in, let me tell you."

"That's bullshit!"

"I feel terrible about it, but I had no idea that the two of you would end up getting involved."

"Don't . . . believe you!"

"It's the truth. Ask her about it next time you see her."

"Next time I see her? I'm bleeding out on a cold basement floor in Woodside."

"Not if Lulu has any say in it," I assured him as she continued to tug on the knot with all her tireless might. "Just point it and what?"

I'd lost him again. I shook him by the arms. "Just point it and what? The SIG. You said just point it and . . . ?"

"Squeeze," he said weakly. "Safety's off. Damn, those sirens are still a mile away. He'll be gone. Dude, you can't let him get away or it'll get real ugly."

"Forgive me. You don't consider *this* real ugly?"

"It jumps a little. Aim low."

"I'm not going to shoot him, Lieutenant."

"Don't have to. He's . . . hiding behind his truck. Just shoot out his back window. That's not Old Betty you're holding."

"Old *Betsy*."

"It'll take out his windshield, too, before it slams into the garage wall and-and covers him with so much shattered glass, it'll scare the crap out of him. Buy us . . . some time until they can . . ." He let out a groan of pain. "I'm counting on you, dude. Don't let me down."

"Wouldn't think of it, Lieutenant." I inched my way up to the top step, poking my head up. Once again, Frank took a shot at me. Once again, he missed. Quickly, I fired off two shots at his truck with the SIG, hearing no sound of broken glass as I ducked back down.

"It jumps, like I said." Very's voice was getting weaker. A lot weaker. "Aim lower and . . ." He gulped for breath. "Steady it with your left hand."

I poked my head up again, ducking as he fired at me. Then I steadied the SIG with my left hand and fired off three quick shots. The first two were misses. The third one blew out Frank's back window and windshield, covering him with shattered glass.

"Good job . . ." Very's voice was barely more than a whisper now as the sirens drew closer. I was afraid he was about to go into shock. But he had two things working in his favor. He was incredibly fit and tough. And he had the best improvised tourniquet on earth. "I'll . . . make a pro of you yet."

I poked my head up again. Frank was crawling around to the driver's side door and opening it from his knees. "He's making a break for it, Lieutenant,"

I said, firing off two quick shots at the door as he jumped in.

I didn't hit him. Didn't hit the door. Didn't hit anything. Let's get real here. I'm the first major new literary voice of the 1980s, not Dirty Harry Callahan.

Frank started up the truck with a roar, hunching low over the wheel. Then he backed out into the apron of the driveway, swung around, made a burnt-rubber Y-turn, and put it in gear as I heard the sirens draw near. They were just a few houses away now.

"A tire . . ." Very gasped. "Shoot out a tire."

I took aim at his right front tire, the one that was closest to us, and fired at it twice. Hit it with my second shot and put a hole it. Not that he was going to let that stop him. As the tire rapidly deflated, he steered the Ram toward the driveway and, he hoped, freedom. But today wasn't Frank O'Brien's lucky day. He hadn't gone more than four feet before another car, his white Chevy Caprice, came up the driveway and blocked his path. There were two women in the car—his wife, Sharon, and his sister, I assumed. Frank pounded his steering wheel in total frustration before he put his arms around it and ducked his head in defeat.

Sharon stared, wide-eyed, at the Ram's shattered windshields, the flat tire, the trail of Very's blood on the pavement leading toward her basement. Then, as the sirens converged out front, she climbed out from behind the wheel of the Chevy, a chubby middle-aged blonde wearing gray sweatpants, a St. John's hooded sweatshirt, and sneakers. Frank's sister, who I couldn't make out very well from my basement stairwell perch, stayed put in the car.

Sharon stood there with her hands on her hips, glaring at her husband as an EMT van sped up the driveway and came to a stop right behind her Chevy. "Francis Donahue O'Brien, would you please explain to me what in the holy hell is going on here?" she demanded.

He raised his head in weary resignation. "Honey, I messed up real bad," he confessed.

"Ya think?" she blustered as the two-man EMT team jumped out of the van.

"Okay, what have we got?" one of them called out.

"Down here!" I hollered. They approached the basement steps double time, toting a medical bag. "This is Detective Lieutenant Romaine Very," I informed them. Very wasn't doing any talking. He'd passed out. I pulled his shield from his rain jacket and held it up for them to see. "Frank shot him in the thigh. It's a bleeder."

"You tie it off?" one of them asked me as they hurried down the stairs.

"As best as I know how."

"Well, what have we got here?" the other one asked as Lulu let out a low, protective growl. "I've never seen a canine tourniquet before." They crouched over Very. "Dang, you did a good job, too. It's okay, doggie. We're the good guys."

"Lulu, you can let him go now," I assured her as she backed slowly away, her front paws and muzzle drenched in Very's blood.

One of them cut Very's blood-soaked jeans away while the other applied a surgical tourniquet. Then they sprinted back to their van for a stretcher, lowered it down to the basement, put him on it, and hustled Very out of there.

I followed them to their van as they loaded him inside. One stayed in back with him, the other slammed the back door shut and got in behind the wheel. "Where are you taking him?" I asked.

"The nearest hospital," he told me. "Elmhurst. He's lost a lot of blood. But we'll start stabilizing him and they'll get him in the OR right away. I like his chances. I think you and your little pal saved his life." He grinned down at Lulu.

"She's not little, she's short."

"Whatever you say, champ." He backed down the driveway, pulled out into the street, and floored it for Elmhurst Hospital, siren blaring.

Two blue-and-whites had pulled up behind Very's sedan out front. Four patrolmen came striding up the driveway toward me now, all of them young and husky.

The first thing that one of them said to me was "Sir, put the weapon on the ground *now*!"

I'd been so focused on getting Very off to the hospital that I'd forgotten I was still clutching his SIG. Or that the sight of Lulu with her blood-soaked muzzle and front paws might arouse some alarm.

"No problem, Officer." I set it carefully on the ground and kicked it toward them. "I'm the one who hollered for the neighbors to phone it in. I was with Detective Lieutenant Very when he got shot."

One of them raised his eyebrows at me. "That was Ro Very who they just carted out of here?"

"Yes, it was. And that's his weapon. He got shot in the leg, a bleeder. Can you notify his captain at the two-four?"

"It'll be taken care of. Why do *you* have his weapon?"

"He kept slipping in and out of consciousness. Asked me to shoot out the front tire of the suspect's truck so that he couldn't escape before you got here. Frank O'Brien is his name."

"And did you?"

"Yes, I did. I took out his windshield and back window, too. But, as it happens, it's actually his wife who stopped

265

him cold with her Caprice. She's currently in the process of making him sorry beyond belief. Come and see for yourself," I suggested.

They didn't care too much for that idea. Just stood right where they were, stone-faced.

One of them picked up Very's SIG by the barrel and sniffed it. "It's been fired, all right. What were you and Lieutenant Very doing here?" he asked me.

"And, by the way, who the hell are you?" asked another.

"I'm Stewart Hoag." I produced my wallet in case anyone wanted to look at it. No one did.

The most baby-faced of the cops, who looked like he still belonged in high school, said, "Stewart Hoag, the writer?"

"I'm afraid so."

"It's an honor to meet you, Mr. Hoag. I thought your book was great. I did have to look up a few words like *concupiscence* in the dictionary, but, damn, it was really good stuff."

"Thank you. I'm glad you enjoyed it."

"You used to be married to Merilee Nash."

"Yes, I know."

"And you got yourself mixed up in the Addison James murders over the summer. Lieutenant Very caught that case, too." My literary admirer looked down at Lulu, who was gazing up at him with her head tilted to one side like

Nipper, the dog from the old RCA Victor ads. "Hey, is your dog okay?"

"Fine. I applied a tourniquet to Very's leg with my belt and she tugged on the knot for dear life. That's his blood she's got on her."

The one patrolman who hadn't said anything yet narrowed his gaze at me in a distinctly chilly manner and said, "This is starting to sound awful screwy."

"Well, if you really want screwy," I said, "then come on back and give a hearty NYPD welcome to Frank O'Brien, who confessed to us before he shot Very that he's the one who knifed George Strull outside of George's apartment on West Eighty-Second Street at two thirty this morning. They were both doormen in my ex-wife's apartment building on Central Park West, the one where a wealthy elderly lady named Muriel Cantrell was shoved down a flight of stairs to her death on Halloween night. According to Frank, it was George who killed her. Frank caught him standing over her body clutching her pocketbook. It was common knowledge in the building that Muriel always carried a lot of cash. George offered to split the proceeds with Frank if Frank would keep his mouth shut. Frank told us he declined. He didn't want to be a partner in crime with George, who was a drinker and compulsive gambler. He figured that George would paint him as the fall guy if the shit ever hit the fan. So when George got off duty early this morning, Frank gutted him."

"Why'd he do that?" asked the patrolman who'd ordered me to drop the SIG. "Why didn't he just call us?"

"We wondered about that, too."

"And . . . ?"

"And he told us that when he was growing up his father taught him to never rat out a union brother, even if he didn't like him. That a man's supposed to take care of his trouble himself. So that's what Frank did. Honestly? His reasoning sounded to me like something out of an old Jimmy Cagney movie. But Frank's old school."

"Okay, let's go have a look," he said grudgingly.

Frank's sister was still sitting there in the Chevy Caprice. She didn't look healthy at all. Her complexion was sallow, and she had dark shadows under her eyes.

Sharon was standing by the open driver's side door of the Ram with her arms around Frank, who was seated there behind the steering wheel, sobbing. Note to social historians: the borough of Queens seemed to have no shortage of large, weepy men that day.

Two of the patrolmen approached the truck.

"Gun!" my baby-faced literary critic called out. "It's on the seat next to him!"

"It's okay," Frank said quietly, sniffling. "I won't touch it."

"Damned right you won't," his partner said, flinging open the passenger door and snatching it from the seat by the barrel. "You're Frank O'Brien?"

"I am."

"And is this your residence?"

"Yes, it is."

"Are you Mrs. O'Brien?" he asked Sharon.

She nodded, wiping tears from her own eyes.

The other two patrolmen followed the trail of Very's blood to the cellar doors and then down the steps to the blood-soaked basement floor and the mess that had been left behind, including bloody surgical towels, Lulu's bloodied duck-billed rain cap, and what had once been my favorite belt.

"I don't know what got into me, Mr. Hoag," Frank said apologetically. "I panicked, I guess. Is Lieutenant Very going to be okay?"

"I certainly hope so for both of your sakes—mostly his."

"Give us some room, please," my literary fan's partner said to Sharon, gently guiding her away from the door of the truck. "Okay, Frank, I want you to step out slowly. Keep your hands in plain view."

Frank did as he was told.

"Now put your hands behind your back," he ordered Frank, removing his handcuffs from his black leather garrison belt.

"Do you have to cuff him like that?" Sharon protested. "He's no criminal."

"All due respect, ma'am, but he just sent a police officer to the emergency room with a serious gunshot wound."

"I'll go call this in," the kid said.

"Do that," his partner said as he cuffed Frank. "Tell 'em we need a crime scene unit and some backup to secure the perimeter."

The kid hurried down the driveway to call it in from their blue-and-white.

His partner gripped Frank firmly by the arm and started leading him away from the truck. "You're not going to give me any trouble, are you, Frank?"

"No trouble," Frank said woodenly as they started toward the driveway.

"Where are you taking him?" Sharon demanded.

"To the 114th Precinct house on Astoria Boulevard."

"I'm going to follow you there," she said, heading toward her Caprice.

"By all means." He looked at the other two patrolmen. "You guys bring in Hoag and his mutt, okay?"

Lulu snuffled indignantly at him.

"What's *her* problem?"

"She doesn't like to be called a mutt."

"Don't have time for any bullshit right now," he blustered as he walked Frank down the driveway, the neighbors watching from the windows of the brick house. Frank's head was down, his shoulders slumped. Gone was that cheery, apple-cheeked doorman who used to greet me every day with a twinkle in his eye, proud of his uniform, proud of his job. That man no longer existed.

Sharon started up the Caprice, which I can assure you definitely needed a new muffler, and backed her way slowly out, leaving me there with the other two patrolmen, who'd made their way from the basement to the garage to have a look at all of the broken glass. As I stood there, I felt a sudden, powerful wave of emotional exhaustion wash over me.

They walked back toward me, one of them studying me with concern. "You okay, Mr. Hoag?"

"I really don't know how to answer that."

"If it's Lieutenant Very you're worried about, don't be. He'll be getting super medical care. Right now, we need for you to come with us to the precinct house so you can make a formal statement."

"Sure. Whatever you need. But before we go, I'd like to call his girlfriend and tell her what happened."

271

"You can do that from the precinct house," said his partner, who was the chilliest of the bunch. "Come on, let's go."

"The thing is, I *really* need to use the bathroom."

"Oh, sure. No problem," the friendlier one said. "We'll wait for you right here."

"Thanks, I'll just be a minute."

Lulu followed me in the back door. I was anticipating the narrow, cheerless hallway. But the extreme, circa-1953 dinginess of the kitchen was so Kramdenesque that it took me by surprise. I half-expected to see an old-fashioned icebox in there instead of one of those new-fangled electric refrigerators. There was a wall phone. Lulu paced around in there, leaving bloody paw prints behind on the worn linoleum floor, while I called Norma's direct number at the publishing house.

When she picked up, I said, "Norma, it's Hoagy. Don't say a word because I only have a second. Romeo's been shot in the thigh. He lost a lot of blood because the bullet hit his femoral artery. They have to operate on him." She let out a gasp as I kept right on talking. "He's at Elmhurst Hospital in Queens. He'll be going into surgery soon, so there's no need to rush right over there, but he'll be glad to see your face when he wakes up. And, listen, if he asks, you and I didn't. Sleep together, that is. I was just trying to piss him off so he wouldn't pass out."

Then I hung up the phone and snuck a peek through the frayed curtains over the kitchen windows that faced the garage. The two cops were still standing back there, waiting for me.

I looked down at Lulu. Lulu was looking up at me.

Quietly, we slipped out the front door. Very's battered unmarked sedan was parked right there in front of their blue-and-white. If I knew how to jimmy and hot-wire a car, I would have jimmied and hot-wired it and sped away. But they don't teach anything that useful in Cambridge. So I hightailed it over to Roosevelt Avenue on foot, my hands buried in the pocket of my trench coat, my fedora low over my eyes. Lulu matched my pace, even though I'm sure she was exhausted from her ordeal of keeping Very alive. When we got to Roosevelt, we hung a left and found the 52nd Street-Lincoln Avenue subway station. The man in the ticket booth gave me a token and a rather strange look in exchange for my $1.25, and we caught the No. 7 to Grand Central. I found a seat and slumped there with Lulu at my feet, noticing that the other passengers were giving me that same strange look. I finally realized it wasn't just Lulu who was carrying traces of Very's blood. My trench coat was spattered with it. There'd been so much else going on that I hadn't even noticed.

When we got off at Grand Central, I took off my coat, rolled it up, and tucked it under my arm before we caught the shuttle to Times Square and a No. 2 express train heading uptown that stopped at Broadway and Ninety-Sixth Street, the familiar old stop for my crappy, unheated fifth-floor walkup on West Ninety-Third. I didn't want to go to Merilee's classy building looking the way my four-footed partner and I did. I also didn't want to talk to anyone there about Frank. Or George. Or Muriel. Not even Merilee. Especially not Merilee. I don't know why.

I only knew that I felt an overwhelming need to be alone and quiet.

So we rode the No. 2 to West Ninety-Sixth Street. Climbed the stairs out of the station onto Broadway and walked to West Ninety-Third Street. My building was between West End and Riverside. As I walked toward it, the cold wind off the Hudson was in my face. I doubt the temperature was more than thirty-five. I thought about putting my blood-spattered trench coat back on but decided I could tough it out. Lulu sped up the closer we got to my building, just as she always did, and was there waiting for me when I opened the vestibule door. Several pieces of mail had collected in my mailbox over the past few days, but nothing that my eyes seemed capable of focusing on. We walked up the five flights to the apartment. I unlocked the door and was quickly reminded that it was the same temperature inside as outside—which is to be expected if your place has no heat and two skylights. I'd grown accustomed to the chill over the years and didn't usually pay it much mind, but I was getting soft living in the lap of heated luxury at Merilee's.

I left my wadded-up trench coat by the door and took off my hat, which was none the worse for what had happened in Frank's basement. I took off the jacket of my barley tweed suit and hung it in the bedroom closet. When I examined the cuffs of my trousers, I was unhappy to find blood spattered on them. I took them off and put them with my trench coat, hoping my dry cleaner, a miracle worker, would be able to save them. My Gore-Tex street bluchers had some blood spots on them. Those I was able to wipe clean with a damp cloth. My shirt and tie were fine.

After I'd stripped them off, I put on a sweatshirt and sweatpants. Got Lulu's towel and shampoo out of the hall closet. Went in the bathroom and filled the tub with six inches of warm, sudsy water. Then I picked her up and set her down in the tub. Sometimes she fights me when I try to give her a bath. But she didn't resist me this time. She was no more happy having Romaine Very's blood on her than anyone else would be. I used a soapy washcloth and dabbed away the dried blood on her muzzle. Then I lifted her paws out of the water one by one and washed between each and every toe. She doesn't like it when I wash her toes. They're very sensitive. But she surrendered to the process. Didn't mind it at all, in fact. Possibly because I kept telling her what a heroic girl she'd been and how she'd saved her good friend's life.

When I was done soaping her, I drained the tub, filled it with clean water, and took a fresh washcloth to her. Then I drained the tub again and dried her off with her towel as thoroughly as I could before she wriggled out of my grasp and escaped to the kitchen, where she sat in front of the refrigerator awaiting her reward. I fed her one, two, three anchovies. Then I poured myself an extremely large Macallan single malt, put some Erroll Garner on the stereo, and sat in my worn leather chair with Lulu's ratty old blanket in my lap, listening to the Elf have his way with "Memories of You." She joined me there on her blanket, her tail thumping as I stroked her, sipped my Scotch, and took the first good, deep breath that I'd taken in several hours, letting it out slowly.

I started to reach for the phone to call Merilee, but I still wasn't ready to talk to her about it yet. I needed to sit there and quietly work my way through everything that had gone down, because I was having a real hard time figuring out who was to blame. So I sat there quietly, turning it over in my mind. Did all of it land on George Strull, the compulsive gambler who'd been driven to such financial desperation that he'd killed Muriel Cantrell for the contents of her pocketbook? I wasn't buying that, because there were so many other people whose hands weren't entirely clean. There was Muriel herself, who'd posed as a lady of wealth and class—making her way around the city in her chauffeur-driven Silver Cloud—when in reality she'd been Albert Anastasia's mistress living off a fortune in illicit mob money that the founder of Murder, Inc., had stashed away for her. There was Muriel's lawyer, Sandy Panisch, who'd inherited the role of her dutiful enabler after his father had died eight years earlier. There was Muriel's dear friend, Myrna Waldman, the widow of a mobbed-up garment industry mogul, who'd enlisted Sandy to help Muriel destroy Olivia Pennington Kates's leather business. There was Olivia's husband, Gary, whose ruthless corporate raids had thrown Frank O'Brien's sister out of work and buried Frank under a huge mound of financial and family pressure. Pressure that had knocked Frank out of his nice, secure comfort zone and rendered him wacko enough that he'd not only murdered George out of some misguided sense of duty but then opened fire on Very and me when we'd shown up at his house.

As I continued to sit there, quietly thinking over everything that had happened since that Halloween party in Alan Levin's apartment, it seemed as if there was an acute shortage of people who had clean hands. There was Raoul, who took a bribe here and a payoff there, not to mention sexual advantage of God knows how many nubile, teenaged housekeepers. There was Alan, who'd messed up a good thing with Gretchen, not to mention a major career opportunity, by having a sleazy affair with Olivia, who didn't give a damn about him. She just liked to play in the dirt.

And then there was me.

Two people were dead, a third was undergoing emergency surgery, and I should have prevented it from happening. If only I'd walked Muriel home to her apartment from Alan's party, like a gentleman, instead of heading straight back to Merilee's place with Very and Norma, leaving her to be preyed upon by George. If only I'd pressed Frank harder the next day about why he was so pissed off at George for showing up late for his shift. Frank was usually so cheerful and amiable. Yet that day he was edgy and irritable. If only I'd asked him why. Would he have told me why? Probably not. Same as Muriel wouldn't have let me walk her home. "I can see my apartment door from here, dear boy. Don't be silly," she'd have said before she shooed me away.

The painful reality was that there was absolutely nothing I could have done to stop what had happened. And yet I still felt as if I had dirt on my hands, and that it wouldn't wash off as easily as the blood between Lulu's toes had. It would just stay there, working its way deep into the pores of my skin.

I didn't feel clean.

That was why I wasn't ready to talk to Merilee yet.

So I sipped my Scotch, listened to the Elf, and stayed quiet, Lulu watching me protectively as she lay curled up in my lap. She could tell that all was not right with me. The nose knows. So she nuzzled my hand with her large, wet black one and climbed up toward my chest so that I'd put my arms around her and give her a hug.

We sat there that way together for a good, long while before I was finally ready to reach for the phone.